Reviews for

'Revolutionary AND Evolutionary' – Marx & Dawkins (licensed grocers – online only).

'Cathartic AND Emetic' – *Boots the Pharmacists.*

'Made me ALMOST seek resurrection' – J. Savile.

'Sectarian AND Bigoted' – *The Tims.*

'Funny; Funny; Funny' – A. Blair (NOT <u>The</u> Blair) (draper's assistant).

'Should be banned AND prorogued' – The Tramp; The Clown and Jake the Rice-Moggy.

About the Author

Ian juggled writing with working as an industrial engineer, an accountant, a university lecturer, an advertising copywriter and running his own management consultancy for 25 years, before 'retiring' at 50… long, long ago.

His 40 years' contracted writing includes:
<u>Television</u> — *Not the Nine O'Clock News*, *Naked Video* and *Spitting Image*.
<u>Radio</u> — *Naked Radio, Six of the Best.*
<u>Stage</u> — 3 plays performed.

<u>Novels</u> — With John Duignan the trilogy *Skelp the Aged*; *The Buick Stops Here*; *The Lambshank Redemption*, all published by Pegasus.

His current 'retired' work includes a recently completed comedy stage play, *Good Times*, co-scripted by Niall

Clark, and his magnum and minimum opus, *The Timing of Pain* and *Drumhumble* - one darkly comedic the latter satirical.

He also golfs (now extremely badly), still gardens (reasonably well) and plays almost respectable guitar with, as ever, execrable vocal accompaniment.

To Kenny & Linda.
For being The best of neighbours
and friends and for all your
support

A GLUTTON-FREE DIET

I.D.C. Hopkins

A GLUTTON-FREE DIET

Pegasus

PEGASUS PAPERBACK

© Copyright 2020
I.D.C. Hopkins

A CIP catalogue record for this title is
available from the British Library

ISBN-9781910903 36 0

*Pegasus is an imprint of
Pegasus Elliot MacKenzie Publishers Ltd.*
www.pegasuspublishers.com

First Published in 2020

**Pegasus
Sheraton House Castle Park
Cambridge CB3 0AX England**

Printed & Bound in Great Britain

Dedication

To the late and great John Duignan, without whom this novella could never have been written.

He will be with me forever and I miss him every day. He taught me well: not just writing, but living, for the forty-two years of our friendship.

Acknowledgements

To the following who generously read early drafts and who guided and encouraged me towards the final product, for which I take sole responsibility.

Pam Airey, Brian Beacom, Campbell Cooper, Donald Donnelly, Frank Donnelly, Sheila Hopkins, Graeme Hyslop, Des McCentee, Marlene Manson, Jim Torbet, Duncan Wilson and last but most certainly not least, Frank Muir for his invaluably experienced 'novelising' advice. To Billy Simpson for the novella's title.

To all at Pegasus, especially — Vicky, Rudite, Tilly, Elaine, Phil and anyone else who makes my writing with them a pleasure, and who I have overlooked or don't know.

A special BIG thanks to Suzanne for sticking her commissioning editor's neck out for me for a fourth time — thanks for your faith, dear lady. I have done my best to repay you.

SYNOPSIS

Set at the time of the Scottish devolution debate in 1997, it is the last golf game of the season to decide the fourball series. **Alec** (aka Alex), an incorrigible wheeler-dealer, is missing for the crucial game. Determined to end the season in traditional fashion, the three remaining members of the quartet, **Jacky**, **Brian** and **Richard**, trace him to the isle of Arran, where he always seems to be just a good four iron ahead of them. The increasingly frustrated trio end up, among other things, doing a burial; two of them do not get to set spikes on a golf course; one of them — the one you would let your mother meet — gets arrested for burgling Brodick Castle, offences under the *Plants and Trees (Preservation) Act (Scotland)* and vicious battery of the police force with a haggis supper. To their further disadvantage, they become entangled with two women who have a score to settle against one of their number and others against the country, the government and *Man*kind.

The story takes place against the background of the New Labour government unveiling its proposals for a Scottish Parliament. The protagonists, in their own ways, represent the major contemporary influences in the debate: the nature and scope of devolution; the spin with which it must be represented to keep from power the nasty Nationalists; the fear of the unknown which strikes at the heart of the average Scottish voter who will invade foreign lands in the cause of the ineffectual football squad, but baulks at taking full responsibility for actions at home (Praise the Lord for *Reserved Powers*); and the significant pocket of civic cynicism that dreams of escape to a place in the sun.

Character Profiles

JACKY: Late forties; terrier-like; brash/pushy; with a wife and a family of three and a degree in Economics — Third Class Honours, the kiss of death, thus UNemployable with a capital UN. Lives for his annual golf series with the others. Is yet to win a series, but this could be the one. Suffers from the same bipolar disorder as his golf swing. He doesn't listen, but eventually reveals his one (he thinks) neurosis.

BRIAN: Of interrupted education, he is a natural at golf and every other activity that requires hand-eye co-ordination, particularly sex and drinking. Unmarried, he has the opportunity to be a golf club pro in Germany, but cannot face the certain opprobrium of the others if he tells them. A decade younger than Jacky, he allows himself to be led until he has to be. Has promised to have Jacky's handicap into single figures before one of them dies.

RICHARD: MAIN CHARACTER through whose ever-opening eyes this Long Weekend we see the tale. Accountant, rapidly departing his thirty-ninth year. He is comfortably divorced; provides a touch of respectability to the group. Calm, a bit sardonic, he becomes excitable, aggressive and ultimately distressed after a glass of flat warm beer. Has a professional relationship with Alec; that gets him a game; that and his motor car. He is English and has a secret morbid fear involving water.

MORAG: In her middle thirties, she is from an upper middle-class background, educated but frustrated by her life and her job as a primary school assistant head. She has recognised Brian as someone from her past who has left a lasting impression. To her chagrin, he does not reciprocate. She adopts the persona of a Glasgow harridan in response to this sleight and swears revenge for this and an additional past wrong. She is all the while in a leg plaster cast.

MHAIRI: Of similar age and background to Morag and a subordinate colleague at the same primary school. She takes her lead from Morag, and revels in the temporary new-found freedom of playing the part of a woman of coarse tongue and questionable sexual mores. With Morag, she is on an illicit mission to the island involving native ecology.

UNDERTAKER: In his late seventies, he doubles as fence-builder and undertaker to the older Arranites. Shit stirrer who likes a dram and the sound of his own voices.

NEVILLE: An eighty-plus-year-old local worthy and first experiment in care-in-the-community on the island; thinks he is the Duke of Arran; has taken to illicitly entering Brodick Castle for a night and, entertaining unsuspecting and gullible tourists to the island. He is harmlessly mad, but Richard is convinced of his lineage.

.

List of Chapters.

Chapter 1

Big Dick

His shoulder shiver became a full body shake as he reached the edge. To most people the sight would have been pleasant, inviting. To him it was his worst nightmare. In close-up. Defeated yet again, he slunk back.

Richard Watling still could not swim.

But that was yesterday.

Richard used to like early mornings, but not since he had bought this 'exclusive Clyde-side executive apartment', not since he convinced himself that this would finally force him to learn to swim. Every early rise had yielded nothing in these past few weeks but greater guilt feelings about the expensive rent, the mounting disaffection with his life and his diminishing self-esteem, inevitably triggered each day by the early-morning failures to swim.

Helplessness in the face of his one Big Fear.

Yes, he still could not swim. He had not even managed to get wet once in the weeks he had been unable to force himself over the side and into the plush basement temperature-controlled pool before any of the other fifteen key-holding residents had stirred.

But today, never mind all that, he nearly convinced himself: because this morning was special. He was *excited*, but also *scared*.

This was very early even for him. It was well before a west of Scotland's October dawn, but not too difficult, he thought, in the week before the clocks went back. Yes, he did feel excitement, he could tell: his right hand was almost shaking as he carefully topped his boiled egg, before dipping his soldier of toast into the perfectly timed yolk with his left. But maybe it was really fear? He had been training himself to be more ambidextrous, less dependent on his right side. It had started as an 'aide de golf' — to buttress against his dominant right side — but was now but one of Richard's many challenges he set himself to get through the increasingly foggy angst of his life.

Well, not 'excited' exactly: 'animated', he corrected himself. As animated as he had been since his wife, Alicia, left him. But this was positive animation. He was positive. Well, nearly. Because deep down was the fear that he had to face today, and in less than three hours. But he shrugged that dreaded prospect and grim vision away yet again and tried to concentrate on the pleasurable side of his ambivalent emotions.

If he was honest with himself, golf was about the only thing he looked forward to since… well, since his wife left him seven years ago — since he volunteered six years past for overseeing the new Scottish branch. There had been many relieved accountants left behind in the large partnership in west London: relieved due to it being

Richard sent into exile, not them — and a few indubitably glad to be shot of Richard and his accompanying personal cloud of gloom bordering on despondency since his wife upped and headed for The Gulf with the firm's most senior partner.

'Captain Oates' they had dubbed him at his farewell bash. And now he had been 'some time'. And still counting.

He re-corrected himself again. Golf *was* his *only* pleasure and this day was *special.* Hence the *genuine excitement.* The 'accountant's training in precision', he smiled to himself. He always experienced a palpable frisson before the monthly golf match, and a longing for the next tussle almost as soon as it was over.

If he had really been honest with himself, he was utterly lonely. Always had been. From the irrevocable and indelible shock of boarding school at eight, through the total bemusement of marriage at twenty-five, to estrangement then abandonment and eventual divorce at thirty-two, to the present feeling of isolation, not to mention alienation in an alien nation, and now he was thirty-nine. Luckily, there was no issue — of the progeny type — but plenty still with his ex-wife Isobel and her new partner, the very senior ex-partner.

He extrapolated this just-discovered seven-year cycle and shuddered at the vision that suddenly materialised of himself: Richard Watling, at forty-six years of age.

He would be eternally grateful to his most important client, Alex Davidson, for inviting him to be his partner in that first fourball match nearly five years ago. Richard had been more than reluctant to play, to participate: most of his golf — a game he had taken up less than a year after his self-banishment in the west of Scotland — had been at first light or last light and always alone. He then did not feel he would ever be ready or adequate enough for golf in company, with witnesses, despite the many secret lessons from the ever-patient and now considerably richer golf-teaching professional at his club.

But now their monthly fourball — always he and Alex against Alex's old school chum Jacky and his younger partner Brian — was a regular match, and today was the culmination of their annual series: their annual 'faraway day'. And this time it was a decider! A decider to this year's series that stood tied at five matches all.

Richard quickly folded and stowed the power caddy, heaved in the battery, then struggled his large red and white pro bag into the boot of his Lexus estate. He was whistling a medley from his favourite opera, *The Mikado*, but stopped abruptly before the *three little maids* 'got to' *school* as he suddenly began to panic.

Where was it? That note of Jacky's…? Richard panicked further. He struggled and puffed the heavy golf bag back out of the long, deep boot to stand it upright. Eight pockets and three secret security compartments later, he found it. This new address — well, the two streets and their corner — Jacky had written for him. Thank goodness he had remembered to keep these co-ordinates in his golf bag. '*That way you won't forget, Dicky.*' He still heard

Jacky's last words. Didn't do to upset Jacky, Richard reminded himself.

Jacky did not need help in that department.

Chapter 2

Wee Jacky

Jacky Montgomery hated mornings. He hated getting up with *Nothing* to do for a whole day. And 5.30 a.m. would normally be rubbing it right in — he rarely saw nine in the mornings. He also really hated Fridays. Not only had he lost that 'Friday feeling' — a feeling long lost some twenty-three years ago with his first and short-lived last job — but now Friday was the too immediate precursor to the weekend with the wife and three big weans under his feet and in his hair, then all four up his nose by Sunday night. (Jacky's Friday Feeling was most people's Monday Moaning.) It wasn't as if he hadn't tried to find work. The government's various Back to Work schemes had seen to that, if he wanted the very much-needed Unemployment Benefit/Job Seeker's Allowance/Giro/Buroo Money/Whatever The Latest PC Label. Truly, Jacky Montgomery BA (Economics) Third Class Honours was, at age forty-seven, inexorably and irrevocably and utterly UNEMPLOYABLE.

Jacky had had trouble sleeping last night, but absolutely no trouble rising. Not this Friday. Not this weekend! Heading for an island paradise chosen by him!

And the decider! And this time he and Brian were going to win. For once!

Jacky just managed to leave his wife gently snoring in their double bed, almost tripped on some electronic toy or charger on the stairs, but made it safely and quietly enough down to the kitchen. He fished the bundle of clothes he had stashed late last night out from under the sink and dressed, watching the shadows of the last leaves slow trickling from the lone tree outlined by the dissipated light from the looming lamp-post. 'Weather perfect, the going good,' he thought, as he grabbed two slices of bread from the bin — the start of a 'piece' of peanut butter he would eat in comfort in Richard's motor. No way was he ramming food down himself this early. 'Uncivilised behaviour' that came under, as far as Jacky was concerned.

Chapter 3

I hate the sound of diesel
in the morning

'You did not doubt me, Jack? Surely not? On time and in the correct spot,' Richard stated, regretting his mildly facetious opening greeting almost as soon as he had made it. He watched Jacky scowl, then toss his ancient half-set of clubs into the boot of the *Lexus* along with a small, tatty holdall, the boot light pointing up the scrapes and scars on both bags. A guitar in a cheap, plastic, dark chocolate-coloured case followed quickly.

Jacky was ignoring him. This was not unusual, unless Richard offered him an obvious response. Usually, Jacky never shut up when offered a response. Richard decided upon a more conventional social nicety as he surveyed the seas of council terraces with their dirty roughcast highlighted by the amber street lights.

'Which house is yours, then, Jack?'

'None of them.'

'But…'

'Do you think I would live in a dump like this?'

'Jack, I would have picked you up at your door. You only had to ask…'

'And wake the whole house with that racket? What con man talked ye into buying a diesel?' With that, Jacky jumped into the back seat and began a slow, dramatic opening of his piece, leaving Richard to close the boot and drive the both of them to Brian's.

Chapter 4

The half-life of Brian

'Brian! Brian! Come oan. Get up. The ferry's leaving!'

Brian McCauslin was having a dream of erotic bliss. Trust Jacky to spoil things. Christ, he was even invading his dreams now, making a bloody racket as usual… Jacky couldn't keep his nose out.

Brian sniffed his. The musky smell… this was no dream. He raised his head slightly and winced, moaning softly, then opened what he hoped was his less painful eye.

What a load of keech that was about the downside of oral sex being 'the view'. This was a most wonderful sight…

Brian wondered who it belonged to and how it had got into his bed.

'C'mon, ya lazy, useless lump! Get up!' Jacky again, that must be Jacky hammering the door. Really hammering the door… REALLY.

'Fuck!' Brian came to.

'Oh yes, please, Brian, doll.'

He crawled out of bed with great difficulty and, with monumentally greater difficulty, ignored the further inviting murmur of the now-abandoned, sleepy siren.

It was Friday. Already? The bloody decider! Brian's gut tightened and churned noisily, a lot more than usual, even after a heavy night. Aw, naw! And he had to tell them. All three of them. And especially Jacky… How was he going to tell them? He had to. Tell them… this weekend.

He had put it off for too long.

Chapter 5

Two into loo won't go

'Hurry up, Mhairi! I am fair bursting! It's this damned cast,' Morag Fairfield said, as she hopped and clumped outside the one, bathroom door.

Morag, not for the first time, wished she had never invited Mhairi Kearney to move in to share her flat. For one thing, she would never have broken her leg, tripping over Mhairi's blasted, monster *Gucci* bag and tumbling arse over tit down the stairs, for one thing... but she was her best friend, and despite Mhairi's brave front, Morag knew she had been devastated by her Sugar Daddy's death. And Mhairi had had nowhere to live when her old, dead lover's family immediately threw her out of their legacy. Mhairi was going to fight them — 'the palimony route' — but a civil suit took money, more money than a primary teacher's salary could accrue. More money than their joint teachers' salaries would ever risk, but money they both would considerably add to this weekend if things worked out.

But Mhairi did hog the loo. Every morning, it seemed. Every morning for these last six months.

'Two ticks, Morag. Hey! You've hidden "the single-girl's friend" I see. Tut, tut. Trust is all between inchoate business partners, you know.' Mhairi Kearney pulled the bathroom door open, still brushing her teeth with her electric toothbrush. 'Mind you, this might do.' She waved the still-whirring brush. 'At a *push.*'

Morag laughed, squeezed past her pal, hobbled in and shut the door.

'I am really excited about this island adventure. Our joint-adventure, you might say,' Morag said, through the door.

'Vibrating are you, Rag?' Mhairi's throaty chuckle came back.

'Wonder how much we'll be able to regale the staff-room with come Tuesday?'

'Not too much, I hope. The law being what it is… Cheers!'

'Is that the last of the Pinot Noir? At six in the morning, Vas!'

'Just tidying up, Rag… Here's to staff training days… and long weekends.'

'Cheers!' Morag gurgled through her mouth rinse.

Chapter 6

Lexus amphibious

Richard wished at least one of them was awake, even if it was Jacky, even if it was Jacky in his normal role of 'back-seat driver'. Both Richard's passengers were sound — the heavy breathing of Brian beside him and the light snoring of Jacky behind conspiring in an odd passenger duet, almost a harmony to add to, if not underscore, the mounting apprehension fuelled by a deep-seated fear in the driver. He just refrained from nudging Brian awake or honking the horn or braking suddenly, or whatever it would take for 'live' company.

Jacky had finally shut up as they skirted the town centre of Paisley, busying now with early workers, and by the village of Howood the just discernible empty open country and swaying road had nodded Brian off. On entering Dalry, Richard's determined concentration to follow the town's tricky twists and turns was broken by the first sign for Kilwinning. He could not help his frisson, then the shudder of embarrassment, still warm six years later. He felt the colour rise in his cheeks…

As ever, driving and navigating never came easy to Richard. He had had to stop on the way to a client in Ayr, having taken a wrong turn and lost himself in Kilwinning.

It was particularly difficult for him in the unaccustomed Scottish winter and darkness. It was very early morning, but a light was on in one shop in what appeared to be the main street. It was a café. They would direct him surely to Ayr.

The café was full. Every seat taken, all by manual workers, by the look of the dungarees and boots and the size of the many 'full Scottish breakfasts' that had been heavily promoted by the one huge window sticker. Richard approached the counter crammed with assorted small foodstuffs, but chiefly surrendered to a large pile of cold pizzas that was in danger of toppling. A head in a headscarf and metal hair rollers, completed by a dangling cigarette, suddenly popped up from beneath the counter and demanded, 'Well?'

The owner (he assumed later) grudgingly growled directions to Ayr and made Richard feel guilty for the advice taking up her busy time, so he felt obliged to order a cup of tea. He remained at the counter and could just see her lift the enormous teapot and smiling and chuckling, he observed, over-loudly in retrospect, but needed over the hubbub from the tables.

'I can't help but admire your Leaning Tower of Pizzas.'

She dumped the cup on the last small space on the counter; a little of the scalding contents started to swim towards the pizza pile, but she swiped them away with a suddenly materialised grimy dishcloth and juggled the smoking fag to the side of her mouth to proclaim, looking askance at the 'Tower of Leaning Pizzas', 'Son, this is Kilwinning. It's a fucking wedding cake.'

He had eventually chicaned the Lexus through Dalry, despite the vividly hot memory of the raucous laughter that had resulted from his attempted levity that morning in Kilwinning. Laughing *at* him and the severely southern English accent that he had since learned to modify when isolated and surrounded by Scottish strangers. '*Serves him right*'; '*See they bloody annoying loud English*'; '*that accent — it's like a knife through butter*'; '*aye, cuts right through ye*', he had overheard from several tables as he stood scalding his lips, tongue and throat, in his hurry to leave, and all presumably *not* for his benefit...

Ever resilient, Richard, the foreigner in this strange landscape of north Ayrshire, briefly congratulated himself now that without external or sleeping internal verbal assistance he had found the B road that would eventually lead to Ardrossan.

Now he wished he had stopped in Dalry and asked for the way he did not need. That would surely have woken at least one of the two sleepers. That would have provided, if not company, if not a kind of support, at least a distraction from the ordeal that was now less than half a mile away and getting closer.

The sense of achievement in finding this road all by himself had led to an almost oceanic feeling in him. Oceanic! He almost laughed aloud at the painful irony. Well, more an unaccustomed Joy... well, a rare Peace... well, almost, as he had taken in the passing moorland appropriately swathed in a day that the Irish would call 'soft' and the Scots apparently called 'dreich'. At this point, despite his well-being feeling, Richard would have been forced to settle for 'dull' — the bleak landscape only broken by desultory tufts of rushes that to Richard seemed like artists' discarded brushes, abandoned due to lack of interest or subject.

But then he had seen it. Or rather *them*. The 'dull' day was now *hellish*. The well-being well gone. *Oot the windae*, as he had tried and failed to learn to say authentically, properly.

The car was still more than a mile away when he had first spotted them. The narrow road ahead was just visible as it wound up the small barren hill, but first it obviously had to go through them. As had he. Two of them. Two Black and Evil lakes, or lochs, or lochans, or whatever of *water*, and on both sides of the road. He reckoned it must be a reservoir, and despite never having driven here, he just knew that he would have to eventually turn left to drive between them. If he could. And after all the recent rain, it was bound to be full to overflowing... this road... their road... his road.

But maybe he did not have to.

o. He now slowed enough to make sure he could read the small black and white road sign through an appositely forming mist. He tried not to listen for the Hound of the Baskervilles or an Albyn Banshee that might add the soundtrack consonant to this horror. A lone sheep bleated empathy, but he barely heard it as he made out *West Kilbride* straight on: *Ardrossan* to the left. As dreaded. Richard remembered enough of his morning map-checking to reckon that West Kilbride would be on the coast and that he could turn south there to reach Ardrossan. He would go that way…

'Whit ye daing? Turn back, ya eedjit. Can ye no' read? Ardrossan's tae the left! Through the reservoir and ower the hills. Christ sake… ah'm needing tae stretch ma legs as it is, no be subjected tae an extra, totally unnecessary, half hour.'

Maybe it was the slowing of the car, or some homing instinct in Jacky — he did look and sound like a small puffed-up pigeon sometimes, Richard suddenly thought, approaching hysteria as he rapidly reversed the car on the still-quiet road. Now Jacky was awake, maybe he should simply tell him. Explain?

But he didn't.

Brian, stirred and shaken awake by Jacky's loud moans, was informed immediately and even more mockingly of Richard's directional *faux pas*, then violently thrust back in his front passenger seat by the sudden acceleration of the Lexus as it sped through the reservoir, its over-full dark waters lapping the road on both sides.

'Geez, Richard. Cool the jets, Ayrton Senna! We want to get there in wan piece,' Brian hissed from the side.

'Aye, unlike Ayrton,' Jacky said from the rear. 'Some driver, though, Senna. While he was alive.'

'*Unlike Richard,*' Brian thought, but did not say, quickly looking away from the trickle of sweat on the left side of Richard's face. Brian could swear Richard's left eye was half-closed.

36

By the top of the hill, Richard had fully opened both his eyes. He had managed to obliterate half the black road-lapping horror by fully closing his right. He slowed, breathed out heavily, slackening his grip on the now damp steering wheel.

But as they descended the other side of the hill, he saw IT.

And Jacky, as if knowing of Richard's morbid fear of water — a type of hydrophobia that manifested itself in his proximity to the menace of bodies of deep water — as ever exacerbated matters as he chanted in a childish voice:

'I see the sea. I see the sea... and the sea sees me,' repeating the sea chanty *ad* (and adding to) Richard's mounting *nauseam*.

He was now facing his fear again, this time face on, literally, as he sat at the head of one of the three columns of cars, vans, motorbikes, lorries and a double-decker tourist bus that faced the water's edge at the ferry slipway in Ardrossan's cramped harbour. The fates had conspired to place him there at the head of the two reserved columns, the third and last column being for the 'unbooked'. He wished he had driven either faster or slower, then he would have arrived at a different time and avoided the now unavoidably direct sea view. The other vehicles and their clumps of passengers behind, standing outside, happily chatting, oblivious to the morning chill, would have hidden Richard and his windscreen. He closed his eyes, the sweat now stinging them.

Jacky and Brian had gone to the terminal toilet and were now stretching their legs up the stone steps that would afford them a view of the incoming ferry. Apparently, the last boat last evening from Brodick on Arran had not sailed due to high winds, and thus the first boat, theirs, this next morning from the mainland was not to be found in its overnight dock at Ardrossan as it should. As it should have obstructed Richard's view of the *water*.

When booking this ferry crossing, Richard had thought long and hard about making some excuse, any excuse to avoid his first *sail*. Unlike his father, who had laughingly rescued him, some maternal instinct in his mother knew that Richard was not simply a 'little namby-pamby' and that the legacy was psychologically deep and real of being caught all alone in a flash flood while playing in the stream at the bottom of their long garden in their village in Buckinghamshire. A safe, gentle stream that had turned in four-year-old Richard's mind to a raging torrent, a wall of water — he now thought of it as a *tsunami*, now that he had learned the word through media coverage of recent fatal disasters. Richard's tsunami that came from nowhere and knocked him down and under its turgid, roiling brown surface was to him as real a disaster. No corporeal damage done, but perhaps his mind was irreparable. And so, his mother had defied his father any time the suggestion arose of crossing the channel, or taking a cruise, much to his father's and his elder sister's annoyance and disbelief.

But Richard himself had booked this ferry. Not Jacky; not Brian. If he still couldn't brave entering that swimming pool in his new apartment, then he had thought a breakthrough would come from another source: a ferry crossing. How could he have been so foolish? 'Less than a one hour's sail'; 'You'll be in your car'; 'Not alone'; 'You are not four years old'; and other self-pleading platitudes had guided his hand to the telephone and the call that had reserved this spot. A spot that should not have afforded this view of the water, agitated even in the semi-sheltered harbour by a strong breeze that the half dozen or so seagulls appreciated, allowing them their swoops and climbs away with mouths full of discarded human edibles, sometimes simply the empty man-made containers.

But suddenly the water was filled by a large black and white orca-like shape turning remarkably sharply in the tight little harbour. Richard's release of tension at the visual absence of the too-close water did not last long. The gaping mouth of the ferry disgorged its very few vehicles from its unplanned crossing: one lorry, three cars, a motorbike and an aged, straggling, puffing cyclist.

The reality hit Richard. He would have to drive into that maw, drive over that rusted brown metal tongue-like ramp, and over that *water that he would experience in full close-up.*

'You want me to drive? Come on, Dicky, you're holding up half of Ardrossan.'

Jacky was as impatient as the *Caledonian Macbrayne* deckhand who was continually waving the Lexus to board. Richard had assumed that the first column of vehicles that had already been formed when they had arrived would be invited to board first. But no, it was his. He somehow turned the key in the ignition.

'You okay?' Brian asked him. 'You're awfy white.'

'He'll be practising his sea-sickness,' Jacky cackled in the back.

'Ignore him, Richard,' Brian encouraged. 'Just drive. It's no' the least choppy out there... Jesus, no' so fast!'

Chapter 7

A skite on the ocean wave

The two other passengers who had braved the driving chill on the top deck of the *Caledonian Macbrayne* ferry berthed at Ardrossan could probably have guessed that these three men were heading to Arran for golf. The tallest certainly looked the part, in expensive co-ordinated cashmere and chinos. The smallest was more 'mixed and matched', both in colour and quality, but the generic ensemble still smacked of golf wear. The middle-sized man, if on his own, would not have been conspicuous as a golfer. Perhaps if he had worn hacking jacket and plus fours instead of the too-well-worn and badly crumpled clothes that looked as if they were indeed from that bygone era, his apparel would have been more congruous with the game of golf.

The old couple — husband and wife, by their semiotic silence — watched Brian finish a can of beer and toss it into the oily detritus floating in the harbour.

They left by the stairwell, either in disgust at Brian's behaviour or the incipient drizzle, perhaps both.

Brian followed them downwards, probably hoping that the ferry's bar opened before sailing, Richard guessed.

This had left the top deck to Jacky and himself. Alone together was just that normally, Richard felt. Alone together. Awkward usually. With nothing or very little in common. Only their golf matches. But not today. And for one very good reason, Richard hoped.

Jacky, who was at the rail looking down at the last-minute activity on the quay, began to cackle. It was infectious. A now chortling Richard, almost euphoric with not just the achievement of driving aboard, joined him at the rail. He had quickly but tentatively, on reaching the ship's highest level, tested the view from this top deck. Eureka! The distance to that water seemed more than enough to, to… forget about it!

Both joint cackles and chortles turned to loud laughter. Another two hardy souls ascending to the top deck, about to brave or test the elements, turned at the manic sound that they erroneously took to be alcohol-induced. For once, Richard banished concerns for the feelings of others, strangers. Sartre's *'l'enfer: c'est les autres'* sprang to his mind. Richard's private 'enfer' — hell — was receding fast. Maybe this island holiday would, as they said up here, *'be the making of him'*…?

Eventually, their duetted raucous laughter subsided again to cackle and chortle cum snigger. Jacky leaned further over the rail to shout downwards.

'And check those bow doors while you're down there! Don't want your motor to get wet,' he added out of the side of his mouth to Richard, before starting to cackle again. This re-started Richard's chortle.

Unseen, Brian's head appeared, followed by a hand holding a beer can. He sourly watched the merry pair from a safe distance, then sat on the heavily varnished wooden seat that doubled as a lifeboat.

'Jack, Jack, why are we... you know...?' Richard stopped laughing briefly to ask, as they both turned and leaned their backs on the rail. He could turn his back on *it* safely at this height. They continued their merry double act.

Jacky's right thumb indicated the Ardrossan quayside workers and the ferry crew behind and below. He had difficulty speaking through the cackles as he tried to explain to Richard.

'Because... because they... are going to work.' He laughed normally for the first time. 'We...' He started to laugh again, but just managed to control it. 'We are off on the skite.'

'Ah! The old *Schadenfreude*.'

'God bless you, my child,' Jacky said, then spotted Brian. 'Hey, Brian, *Schadenfreude*, that's German.'

Brian muttered to himself, 'The seminar's started. Always the language thing. Had to be German tae...' He became even more morose. 'A stonewall certainty... Germany.'

'The pleasure gained from others' misfortune.' Jacky was strutting the deck as if delivering one of Shakespeare's better, more comprehensible soliloquies, before bending over the rail to shout down to the workers. 'The best kind! The only pleasure worth shouting about!' He turned, strutted a little more, then stopped, as if struck by a sudden thought.

'I feel it.' Jacky made a passable golf swing. (He was a master of *practice* swings. And conceded putts.) 'I'm good for at least a seventy-eight.'

'An ah wis in the middle o' a sixty-nine when you battered the door in,' Brian growled through a slurp of beer.

'*Croissante-neuf au matin*. Dear, dear,' Richard said quietly.

An oblivious Jacky was approaching euphoria, or perhaps hysteria — the slightly more socially acceptable of his bipolar extremes, Richard felt.

'If this works out the way I'm sure it will... serendipity... kismet... this will be an annual crossing,' Jacky cooed, as he puffed out his pigeon chest in satisfaction.

'Not with you, Jack,' Richard smiled, happy that Jack was happy and happier still with his own present lack of fear. Conquered, he hoped. The ordeal of disembarking was over an hour away and maybe his trauma had been overcome at last, once and for all.

'The knack of making happy discoveries, by chance.'

'No, Jack, I know what serendipity is.'

'Maybe. But I bet you don't know I was using it in its collective sense. Utilising the word's original derivative, quintessentially epistemologically kernalistic expiali-docious meaning.'

Richard was patient. He had been here before. His smile dimmed. Normal relations with Jacky were being resumed, he felt. The word 'prickly' sprang to his mind as he spoke:

'Yes, Jack. Not with you.'

'I wish ah wisnae,' Brian said to the lone seagull sheltering behind his shoulder — too loudly, as his erstwhile avian amigo screeched away and up towards the looming grey darkening clouds.

'I was using *serendipity* deliberately.' Jacky, as ever, would not be put off. 'Appropriately. Appositely. Deliberately, and for a number of reasons. Wan: lucky, Big Alec's uncle dying and living in Arran. Two: felicitous, we hadn't played the decider over your snooty Douglas Park, Richard, where they always find something to criticise me for.'

Richard was now losing not only his joy, at his relief, but his patience; soon it would be his will to live — despite many 'practice sessions' with Jacky — and he decided to risk milking it, as anything was better than another of Jacky's patronising, interminable, didactic rants.

'Yes, remind me, what was it last time, Jack?'

'Eating my breakfast in the car park. I mean, I was late. What was I supposed to do? I cannae eat first thing. It's constitutional. Metabolic. Genetic. Diabolic. What's wrong with them? See committees...?'

'No, Jack, as I recall, it was not so much the eating that upset the committee. It was the *cooking* of it in the car park. And all the little Jacklettes playing sandcastles in the practice bunker, bless them.'

'Anyway, none of that snobbery at Shiskine.' Jacky produced a wee light blue golf guidebook from his hip pocket and waved it in Richard's face. 'Where was I? Aye, Three: *serendipity*. Coined by Horace Walpole from the Persian fairy tale — hence my twinning with kismet — the "Three Princes of Serendip", in which the eponymous heroes possess this gift.' He looked around expansively, eyes crinkling, tight little mouth beaming as widely as it ever would. 'And, ach, call me a romantic fool, but I felt we were like, you know, three princes on the skite.' Jacky mumbled the last as he caught Brian sticking two fingers down his throat to turn away and throw up over the rail. Jacky's face registered his usual disgust and lack of surprise at Brian's behaviour, then continued speaking to a puzzled Richard, who was oblivious to Brian vomiting. 'Next season's venues as well — I've decided we need a change. Put Arran down again. This series needs new challenges. Arran, look out.'

'As it happens, Jack, I agree and have been giving this some thought...'

'Let's leave it the noo,' Brian interrupted Richard as he straightened from the rail and headed for the stairs. 'Let's get this series over wi'. Next year's next year. A lot can happen.' He tossed the empty can over his shoulder and the rail before descending.

'No' to oor series it cannae! It's fixed like the stars in the firmament!' Jacky, running over to the stair head, shouted down at a disappearing Brian.

Richard, not for the first time, wondered at the endemically ostensibly aggressive nature of Scottish male friendship.

Chapter 8

All abroad

Mhairi and Morag entered the deck below. They were prepared for the weather and looked the part of casual but well-to-do tourists: their green, almost matching, showerproof outfits complemented by two tastefully small black holdalls on wheels. Mhairi shouldered a large collapsed rucksack that was obviously close to empty. She deposited the rucksack on the red plastic bench beside a more collapsed Morag, whose left leg was throbbing from taking the strain off of her fully plastered right.

Mhairi extracted the one main item from the large rucksack: a large colour-illustrated tome on rare plants. She went to the rail and skimmed through it thoughtfully, turning down the corner of a couple of pages; but very soon she became distracted by the conversation that was being dripped, sometimes chucked, down from the upper deck. Eventually, she became engrossed.

Jacky was just beginning his loud fulmination against the still-absent Brian.

'I don't know why we bring him: spends half his time getting pished, half chasing his Nat King Cole, and half spewing his ring. And don't mention again what a good golfer he is: it's just innate ability wi' Brian. Where's the merit in that? Christ, if I had half his talent I'd be twice as good as him. Ach, I'm no' going to get upset.' Jacky bucked up and quietened down a little. 'You know, Richard, we're heading for Paradise Island. New horizons. Just like Scotland. The moment of decision. Knock, knock, knocking on freedom's door.'

As if on cue, the ferry's tannoy crackled into life. After some obvious radio-tuning burps and squeaks, a radio newsreader could be heard:

'Over now to Edinburgh. To the former Royal High School for the latest in the Great Debate on Independence. In opening for the Government, it is expected that the Secretary of State for Scotland will argue that the legitimate aspirations of the Scottish people for control over their own economic and political affairs will be best served under New Labour's plans for a power-sharing executive based on the Northern Ireland model. However, this is unlikely...'

Brian came up the stairs, can in hand, scowling. He roared at the tannoy. 'Turn that off! Now!'

The radio stopped. And a voice said, *'Sorry.'*

'Result.' Brian almost smiled.

Chapter 9

Rope and spillage

On the deck below, Mhairi's attention was drawn from the ship's loudspeaker to Brian's roar. Morag, who was looking puzzled at the sudden cessation of the radio broadcast, then noticed Mhairi indicating the deck above. Morag struggled up and clumped over to join Mhairi at the rail. Both craned out their necks in an attempt to see as well as hear those above.

'Brian, you can't close your eyes to History: we Scots are on the brink of great events. Something we'll tell our children and their children's children's children. It'll be like the Kennedy era in America. The Kennedys without the... the sex... the corruption, the bootlegging, the nepotism... the...'

'The bad driving. Look, Jacky, ah better tell yae, I've decided to...'

Jacky interrupted, as usual. 'Brian, don't worry. We'll find Alec. Trust me. Hell's bells, Arran's tiny: there's about four people on it. Isnae any size at a'. Alec'll be delighted to see us. Touched even, at our consideration in his hour of grief. And yes, there are stacks o' boozers. And even some women. Might even be a vomitorium for you. The thing is to prioritise: we find Alec; we do the decent thing and help him bury his uncle; then we get our game in, finish the series and claim the prize.'

Brian made as if to speak, but shrugged and supped from his can as Jacky continued.

'Here's my hypothesis: Big Alec fixed this funeral just tae get out o' losin' the series. Well, nothing is stopping me winning this one. Independence, New Labour, Tony Blair, Big Alec, a deid uncle. Nothing. Five years I've waited for a win.' He almost hugged his golf partner and golf guru, but easily desisted, Brian's early morning and now beery breath acting as a reverse gravitational field — a force not to be reckoned with. 'You and me, partner. We're going to stuff they two...' Jacky turned and grinned malevolently at Richard. 'Scotland tanking the English again.'

'Jack, would you think me altogether too obsessed by petty detail if I were to point out that while yes, I am of the southern persuasion, Alex, while not here to defend himself, is as Scottish as, dare one say it, your good self?'

'What's that got to do with me winning? It's all right for you English: you're used to getting beat. Jesus, you've come to love defeat. It's your national psyche. Whereas we Scots, no matter how many times we get thrashed and humiliated, we come up bouncing and convinced that the next time we're going to win.' Jacky counted on his fingers. 'Zaire, Iran, Paraguay, to name but a couple.'

'You did beat San Marino, Jack. And the Faroe Islanders... once. As I recall.'

'And do you know what? According to the Laws of Probability, we're quite right no' to learn by our experiences; unconnected events is the technical term, Brian.'

'Well, Jacky, then if that's the Law of Probability, the law's definitely shite.' Brian softened: 'Anyway, winnin's no aw it's cracked up tae be. There's more to…'

'Ah! Coubertin's spirit lives on. Not the winning, but the taking part. Most commendable, Brian,' Richard smiled warmly. If asked to decide, he knew he much preferred the company of Brian to Jacky, then tried to remember if the two of them had ever been together, ever alone without the yappings of the little 'chippy' Scottish terrier.

The three of them were now leaning over and looking down at the deck below, where Morag and Mhairi now stared up.

'Aye, very good, Richard,' Brian said. 'No' the takin' part: it's the takin' *apart. Then* winnin': Graeme Souness. Look, Jacky, there's something…'

Jacky, as ever, interrupted Brian. 'A much maligned soul, by the way, Graeme. If there wis mair o' him in Scotland…'

'The rest of us would be walkin' aboot like her wi' the stookie.' Brian pointed down to Morag and her plaster-clad leg. 'Look, Jacky, I've been trying to tell you… I should have…'

Jacky ignored Brian and looked over the rail. 'Feel the sea change.' He breathed in deeply. 'Snock that in, Brian.' He himself breathed in deeper. 'Go on, I insist.' Jacky pressed Brian's diaphragm. Brian reluctantly inhaled deeply through his nostrils and choked and gasped. He quickly balanced his full can on the rail and reached desperately for a fag, which he lit and snocked in the smoke generously, with visible relief. He went to retrieve the beer can, but staggered, struck it and toppled it over the rail.

Chapter 10
Character assassination(s)

The beer can bounced on the deck below, spun, then rattled off the foot-rest attached to Morag's plaster. Initially, it splattered the deck, then rolled about in concord with the slight bobbing of the ferry. Morag glared at it in disgust, then looked up to remonstrate, but was stopped by a grinning Brian leaning over the top deck rail, indicating that she toss it back up to him. Both women dramatically turned away and pretended to read Mhairi's coloured tome.

'Suit yerself, doll!' Brian shouted down, then turned to ignore Jacky's continuing words.

'Fresh air, Brian. Sea-fresh air. Scotland's other natural resource. If we could only bottle it. Wait! Hypothesis two: Big Alec knows all the angles; the dead uncle is just a smoke-screen for some piece of New Scottish enterprise. Bottled Arran Air. Eh... face-packs from Arran seaweed. A million opportunities are being unlocked even as we speak. Aye, Big Alec: what a man. He's done well for himself.' Jacky smiled knowingly and, in mock conspiratorial tone, asked Brian: 'Sure, we can remember when he lived in a shoe box?' Jacky waited, all ten digits curling back into his palms, indicating the required response.

Brian eventually relented, his voice flat and low. 'And you lived in the lid.'

'And?'

'There were nine of you.' Brian's voice was now weary.

'Hmmm?' Jacky, who never wearied of this, prompted again.

'Including the bailiffs,' Brian obliged.

'This homily never ceases to affect me,' Richard lied.

'Aye, Big Alec. Those days, of course, he was just a lowly motor mechanic like any other: always waiting on a part,' Jacky declared with a smirk.

'And now he owns six garages. Where do you think he went wrong, Jacky?' Brian asked. 'And you wi' the Uni degree tae…'

'Six garages! Who'd believe it? It was me that used to do his homework for him.'

'Seven garages actually, as of last weekend. But I mustn't say too much of Alex's affairs.' Richard the Precise should have known better, but could not help correcting them.

'Seven? Here! As his accountant, is that no' a breach of something or other?'

'I was speaking as Alex's golfing partner, Jack. Not as his accountant. Had it been the latter, an invoice would have been winging its way towards you as we speak.'

'Look, Jacky, ye'll find oot sooner or later...' Brian had steeled himself, trying yet again. But Jacky, as ever, was not listening.

'You know that big sleekit toley, Alec, Brian. See, if we don't play this decider...' Jacky turned and pointedly addressed Richard. 'Alec'll have himself convinced that you and him would have won and then tanked us in a play-off. In a month I'll even believe it myself. Remember, Alec is an ex-mechanic: expert in counter-factual history.'

'Ah, history. It was, I believe, Herodotus that defined it as the separation of the outcomes of chance from those of necessity.'

'Richard, that is the kind of literary throwaway line that...' Jacky began, and Brian joined him.

'Should be thrown away!'

Richard coloured but, in his present mood, took no offence, instead almost relishing what he had learned to label 'banter'.

But Brian was determined not to be side-tracked. 'Jacky, look, this is not on. Ah shouldnae be here. Ah...'

'What is up with you, Brian? Whose permission do you need to come to Arran? The child support agency? An independent financial advisor? Your aromatherapist? Brian, you're single. You're with us. It's Friday, and...'

'An' you're crackers, Jack.'

Brian tossed his fag over the rail and headed down to the bar when the other two were not looking.

Brian's burning cigarette end landed and a spreading shower of sparks invaded Morag's feet. Morag's reactive kick was unfortunately with her plastered leg and Mhairi had to quickly grab her to save her from falling over.

'Good God! Have the Magaluf mob switched their affections? Can the rabble have rediscovered their homeland?'

'This weekend might not be quite as tranquil as we had hoped, Rag.'

'Two things in dealing with the yob tendency, Vas: never let their antics get under your skin, and face them down. Under every crude, foul-mouthed Neanderthal male there is a little bullying schoolboy just asking to be slapped down. I've a mind to go up and deal with that lout.'

'But your leg, Morag, it's hardly worth…'

'Oh, stuff my leg. Come on, my dander is up. I can't bear gross behaviour. Time to strike back for decency.'

They made to start the steep climb to the top deck, Mhairi taking Morag's elbow.

Chapter 11

The dustbin of Damocles

'You know, Richard, you're lucky: answerable to no one since your wife ran off with that other accountant.'

'Jack, Jack. Not just any accountant. Senior partner, if you please,' Richard said, still in good form, now almost welcoming these barbs from Jacky that had before struck home far too easily and had added to his general angst. But that was then. Before this early morning's epiphany. He felt a different man. Different. 'Manning up', he mused hopefully, happily.

Jacky spoke as if to himself, 'I just happen to be lucky. The secret of a happy marriage is knowing when and with whom to bugger off.' He paused, reflected, then mumbled, this time more to himself as he looked up to the misty horizon of the Ayrshire hills. 'Anyway, if I phone from the other side, she cannae do anything until I get back.' He suddenly noticed that Brian has disappeared.

'Where is he? No' the bar again. I need him sober — well, soberish. Come on, Dicky boy.'

They left, luckily for them, by the stairs on the opposite side to the ascending Mhairi and Morag.

Seconds later, Mhairi stepped sprightly, and a puffing Morag eventually clumped, on to the top deck.

While the two women did a search, Jacky and Richard entered the lower deck, looked about for Brian, who suddenly appeared and joined them.

The women now realised that the men were below them and as Mhairi leaned over the rail eavesdropping, Morag found a detachable, fairly full litter bin that she now toyed with dropping on Brian.

Brian carried a large, full brandy glass, its surface swilling with the starting departing motion of the ferry. Jacky had not failed to notice.

'Brian, no one can accuse me of being sanctimonious, but there comes a time: a wee bit of restraint is required of all of us. Sacrifice for the team. Mortification of the flesh.' He snatched the brandy glass from Brian, sniffed it and tossed it over the side.

Richard and Brian followed the arc of its path. Brian took a lager can from his pocket and spurted it open under Jacky's nose.

'What a sacrifice.' Brian slumped on the nearest bench. 'That was the double brandy ah owed ye.'

Richard, not for the first time, tried to make the peace between the other two.

'Arran. I was wondering, Jack, what's it like, this...?' And again, not for the first time, Richard tried to parody Jacky's accent and failed excruciatingly. 'Arn. Arrin. Ayran. Iran? Whatever?'

'Typical English. Up here about, what, four, five years...?'

'Almost seven years, Jack. November tenth — was a fine autumnal day, scent of wood smoke at the station. Vandals had set fire to the carriage…'

'Six years. Never been to Arran. Been round all the Greek islands, but.'

'Hardly, Jack. Hardly all of them. There are over two thousand; two thousand one hundred and…'

'Can probably name them. The islanders as well,' Brian spoke to himself as he left for the toilet, then the bar, as he could not yet bring himself to address Jacky after that waste of *Courvoisier.*

'With almost a First in Classics, Jack, should I apologise for not a few field trips to the cradle of civilisation? And I don't mean Edinburgh! Ha, ha.' Richard faced a stone-faced Jacky and felt he had to try to explain. 'Athens of the North, Jack… Greece… Scotland's place at the centre of the cultural universe north of Newport Pagnell.' He was not wrong in assessing the likely results of his provocation. 'Bring it on,' as the Americans say.

'And while you were pissing about the Parthenon, working the oracle at Delphi, arse-licking up Lesbos, you could have been strolling the links at Shiskine. A gem. A twelve-holer. Like original Old Prestwick. Where was played the first, what *you* call, *British* Open.' Jacky was ultra-dismissive as he checked his golf grip and stance. 'Cradle of civilisation. Shiskine's the place.' Now muttering and smoothly swinging his imaginary and favourite seven iron, he went on: 'Should be ashamed.'

59

'Hey, Jacky! Ah've never been tae Arran an' ah don't feel the least bit ashamed!' Brian had returned, open can in hand and shouting from the stair head.

Jacky did not take long before he was in full tirade.

'Naw, you would'nae, would ye? Lived up here all your life. And you never sprinkle sugar on yer porridge. You shovel oan apathy. From fourteen to nineteen, you spread yer holidays between Blackpool and the Isle O' Man. The language wis a bit of a problem at first, but you mastered it after a struggle. Magaluf was a godsend. You could get blitzed without talking at aw!'

Richard watched Brian swallow, burp, then apparently absorb Jacky's observations.

'You know, Jacky, you should be a TV psychologist: you can sum up a person in ten seconds.' Brian paused, took a relatively little sip, for him, from his can. 'When you get right down to it, you definitely are an arrogant wee shite.'

'Pished again.' Jacky turned to Richard and with a half-nod back towards Brian, his dismissal of his friend, golfing guru and partner seemed to Richard complete as far as Jacky was concerned.

'Yer right. Ah know: and the morra mornin' ah'll still be pished an' you'll still be a wee shite.' Brian paused and swallowed hugely, thought, then added, 'Unless devolution changes what evolution couldn'ae.'

Unseen above, the two women watched with interest as Brian stepped to lean over the rail and continue to drink from his can. Morag again hoisted the full litter bin as her friend Mhairi said:

60

'Oh, come, come, Morag. You couldn't possibly know him? Unless you've been leading a double life all these years. Hit him with it.'

'There's something about the body language...'

'The way he chucks the can, or the way he chucks it up? You find that sexy? Kinky, kinky," Mhairi teased.

'And did you see his hand? The nicotine?'

'Nicotine? And I thought that was a tan Versace glove. One lives in hope. Now, Rag, I want you to remember why we're here. To relax.' Mhairi stopped her teasing and spoke very meaningfully and slowly as she lifted her coloured tome. "And... *to take stock.* And please, though I was born and bred in Balljaffray — *upper* Bearsden to you — I swear a bit of rough holds no attraction for me. Guides' honour.'

Morag hesitated for some time with the litter bin still raised. Eventually, she lowered it and hobbled over to replace it. She returned, and again looked down at Brian. 'It'll come to me.'

The weak sunshine disappeared as the sky quickly turned a fully finished black and the near silence of the several swirling seagulls presaged a rumble of thunder. Rain started in earnest and the two friends, fellow primary school teachers and 'business partners' well into their 'joint venture', scuttled and clumped down the stairs, seeking shelter.

Chapter 12

BT phone home

The corner road sign nearest the harbour in Brodick the three golfers stared at displayed *Lamlash* to the left and *Lochranza* and *Blackwaterfoot* to the right. A huge coloured poster tied underneath displayed the whole of the island of Arran in all its majesty (captured on a bright sunny day), with the writ large legend: *Scotland in Miniature*.

A recently disembarked tourist exited the adjacent telephone box, muttering first to himself, then louder to anyone and everyone:

'Bloody place this is… A bus strike… Probably only have wan bus and it has the gall to go oan strike…'

'Which way, Jack?' Richard asked from under his expansive golf umbrella that he was being forced to share with Jacky. Brian was feeling very little, least of all the persistent drizzle.

'Eh… left for Lamlash… right for Lochranza and Blackwaterfoot.'

'Yes, Jack, excellent on the literary test. Another triumph for wider access to Higher Education. Now which way for Alex?'

'Oh, now you've started; which is more than can be said about your big fancy motor. Lying over there in the workshop.'

'The mechanic assured me it'll be fixed by lunch time this afternoon. *"A duddle"*, I believe he termed it; also *"a skoosh case"*, was it?'

Brian, already pissed off at the prospect of actually having to walk upright and unsupported by alcohol, simply shook his head at the solecisms, if not shibboleths.

Jacky, the carnaptious pedagogue manqué, of course could not keep quiet as he sneered, '*Doddle*, ya clown. Doddle: as in "dead easy".'

'Unlike your empirical — ha, ha — sense of direction, Jack?'

Richard's perky outward flippancy had returned now. It helped him overcome a near shudder at the too-recent fiasco he had made of driving the Lexus off the ferry. His peculiar hydrophobia was still there, caused by proximate deep water, and had caused him to disembark too quickly, hit the concrete barrier at the first sharp turn from off the ship's ramp, bash the Lexus and render it temporarily *hors de combat* with a front bumper requiring at least temporary restitution before being capable of being driven again.

'Anyway, Jack, if this island is as small as you say, the exercise will invigorate us. Prime us for the match. Get the blood coursing through the veins, the old competitive instincts honed to razor sharpness. Which way, again, Jack?'

A discomfited Jacky looked to their right at the nearest buildings — mainly formerly grand hotels — of the main street of the biggest island town of Brodick, then looked straight ahead at the road and the steep hill to the next nearest village of Lamlash, as if seeking divine inspiration.

'He came. He saw. He cocked up.' Brian burst a can of lager and swallowed half of its contents in two and a half gulps. 'Ye sure ye come from Ardrossan, Jacky? Or more *germane*, as you would say — ye ever been to Arran before?'

Morag and Mhairi passed just then, wheeling their holdalls, Mhairi with the large collapsed rucksack over her shoulders and back. As they passed alongside, Morag had a good look at Brian, then stopped in mid-hirple and bent to pretend to adjust her plaster cast and foot rest.

'Morning, ladies.' Brian perked up.

They cut him dead and walked and clumped on.

Brian began to whistle the theme tune from *The Archers* in time to Morag's awkward lurching limping. She stopped and went to turn to remonstrate, but was dragged away by Mhairi.

'Did you see that, Richard?' Brian gazed smilingly after the two women. 'Some things never change, politics or no. Animal magnetism. Fatal attraction. Nothing to do with race, religion, creed, skin colour, educational achievement, or sexual orientation. It's classless and odourless and it knows no artificial boundaries. And no politician can change it. Give it any name you like.'

'Satyriasis?' Richard asked with a little smile.

'You've got it!' Brian laughed.

'No, you've got it, Brian; but soft, our leader doth speak,' Richard said, looking down almost benevolently on wee Jacky, who was scratching his head à la Stan Laurel.

'I don't understand it: I told Fiona to phone Alec. Tell him to meet us off the ferry. I distinctly *told* her.' Jacky was now beyond indignant. Jacky's mood changes were at least as fast as the speed of fright. Or flight. Sometimes fight. Well, nearly.

Richard was simply aghast. 'You told Fiona! Mrs Alex! But she treats you and Brian like something she has picked up on the sole of her LK Bennett loafers. Tell me, Jack, what was her response? No, let me guess — the horsewhip, public castration and combined vasectomy, or the Vagrancy Act? In which case, there is no chance of you having got the address of this allegedly dead uncle.'

'Ach, It's a wee place, Arran. Everyone knows everyone else. But we can save time.' Jacky pulled out some change from his pocket. 'There's a phone box; give Fiona a ring and get the address. She'll speak to you. She nearly likes you. She's a snob. No class.'

Richard made a big play of being horrified and reluctant, as Brian planked[1] himself on the convenient sandstone wall of the impressively big hotel, to increase the pleasure from the penultimate dregs from his last can of, by this time, not anywhere nearly strong enough lager.

Jacky's eyes skewered a still stock-still Richard with over-cod contempt and orated dramatically: 'The modern

[1] Scots for 'plonked

65

male, courtesy of makeover television, spends his time in the kitchen sautéing up a nice little Eggs Benedictine that he and his little group can nibble, all the while wondering how to get on *Watercolour Challenge*. It always comes to this: I do everything for you two. If it wasn't for me, Richard would be nice and safe at the office and Brian would be... well, would be, Brian. Christ, what future Scotland wi' this lot? All we need is women to take over the new assembly... serve them right.' He looked up to glare even more directly at Richard. 'Give us the money, Dick. I'll do it. Fiona doesn't frighten me.'

Richard was somewhat bemused since he had never taken the money from Jacky, but nevertheless took coins from his pocket and handed them over. Jacky stepped towards the phone box, but was thwarted by Mhairi, who suddenly materialised and just beat him to it. Morag, with an *en passant* haughty look, eventually fast-clumped past the three men and, with ever more difficulty, squeezed in beside her friend in the old phone box and stuck out her tongue at a fuming Jacky.

Jacky pocketed the money and turned to the other two with resignation.

Brian rose from the wall. 'That's it. I'm on the boat back. Nest, here ah come.'

'Nest! Nest? That all you think about? Look at that!' Jacky pointed dramatically past the docked ferry and the last lopsided, suit-cased, or erect and rucksacked passengers back to the mainland. A rising wind helped them aboard as the ship's hooter blasted either a welcome or a chastisement for their tardiness. Richard laughed to himself, thinking it would take more than this *Caledonian Macbrayne* foghorn to drown out dear Jack or stop him from putting what Richard's Connecticut cousin called 'closure' on Jacky's affectionate rant at Brian:

'Cast your skelly bloodshot eyes over that and don't tell me the nest beats that. Boat home, my arse. I never get tired of that view.'

The three of them stood abreast, looking up and out to the left of the ferry, Brian just avoiding the nearest spoke and the minor cataract from the outside of Richard's outsize brolly as he commented:

'Yer memory must be good. Can see bugger-all. Bloody rain.'

'Rain? Rain? That's no' rain. Mist. If you can see the trees, it's mist. Anyway, it's Brodick. Supposed to be wet. Prevailing winds. Goatfell. Mountains. Gulf Stream. Chernobyl. Acid *mist.* Anyway, we're heading for Shiskine, the sunny side. Smell that air. No dirt there. Listen to that noise: silence. This is Scotland, clean and quiet.'

'Deid!' Brian spat, then sadly finished his can of lager in one brief draining gulp.

'Wrong again, Brian. You are going to love this place, trust me. Arran affects everybody that sets foot on it. You'll be in tears when you're leaving. It's working already: you're slowly changing your tune — there's a subtle softness to your usual snarl. And you, Richard, why, you'll be so enchanted you'll compile a recipe book based on island produce. You might even learn the language. And think about it: an island retreat where we can relax;

consider affairs of state; concretise our views and aspirations for the New Scotland. A spiritual retreat. For Protestants as well… This is definitely on the circuit for next year. Paradise Island! Another stoating idea. That's hit!'

'Jack, Jack. I fear the technicolour waistcoat is…' Richard was agitated.

Jacky followed Richard's pointing and just caught Brian about to vomit, and steered him rapidly to a lamp-posted, yellow, dog-jobby bin, into which he impressively honked.

The two women in the phone box viewed this with interest. A wobbly Brian, supported by Richard and a reluctant Jacky on either side, took Brian for a short restorative walk.

Morag and Mhairi exited the phone box. Morag clumped to peer in the vomit-splattered bin. Mhairi approached very gingerly, her look decidedly askance.

'Not so much the smoking gun as the steaming reflux. It's him, I swear it. I'd recognise that…' Morag retreated a little and pointed back to the bin, 'anywhere.'

'You know, Morag dear, I've known girls who remember boys by… oh, the music they danced to, the car they drove, the after-shave they never wore, the colour of their boxer shorts — even on the inside and in the morning — but this, this is one for the psychiatrist's couch. Now you've satisfied your curiosity… It'll be dark soon. We better get a room.'

'Not so fast, Vas. I've waited a long time for this opportunity. What's the expression: *vengeance is a dish best served cold*? Well, mine is a veritable permafrost on the Kelvin scale. And I think we can derive not a little fun from this.'

'Well, Rag, don't look now, but here he comes again.'

Morag grabbed her and they quickly backed into the phone box.

Jacky had just shot away from Richard and Brian into the drizzle towards the phone box, but the two women just beat him to it again.

Chapter 13

On a clear day you can't see
The Wolf's Lair

Brian peered into the dog-waste bin as he passed it. 'You're right again, Jacky. That's much better than an enema. The simplest pleasures are the best. That's me ready. Point me towards the golf course, and put a club in ma haun'.'

Jacky ignored his golfing partner and continued to scowl towards the occupied phone box as Richard spoke softly.

'There's the little affair of finding Alec and the dead uncle, remember?'

Suddenly, the sun broke through the cloud departing swiftly in the strong breeze and the rain, as if disappointed, almost stopped at once.

'Ah, brilliant! Told you. There... look at that castle, that view... Aw yes, an' a bit of Goatfell 'n' aw! You wait till ye see it aw!' Jacky jumped on the spot as Richard was reminded of a scene from *Pinocchio* and almost looked for the celestial strings of a heavenly Geppetto.

A few woolly-hatted, kagouled, denimed, thick-socked and heavily-booted walkers descended the hillside, passing by on the opposite pavement. They were puffing hard but earnestly chatting, now smiling in the warming air.

'Good morning,' Jacky greeted them with a salute that would not have got him arrested at a Nuremberg rally in the late nineteen-thirties.

The small group ignored him and passed on towards the centre of Brodick.

'English. Doing Scotland on the cheap,' Jacky declared, then shouted after them, 'Caravannettes in the layby, eh?' He turned to the other two. 'Packed wi' cornflakes and sausage rolls and freeze-dried coffee. No wonder our tourist industry cannae compete. They'll no' buy anything. Bring it all with them. First thing I'd do if I was in power would be a visual tax. Charge them for looking.'

Richard snorted. During these last few years of desultory exposure to Jacky's anti-English barbs, Richard tried to convince himself that the slurs were, deep down, disingenuous, as Jacky, even Jacky, who was many things but not unintelligent, could not truly believe his calumnies and absurd accusations. Richard's charitable side felt that Jacky designed the affronts purely to irk him, Richard, very often to put him off in the golf matches, but Richard was usually eventually baited. Like now. And was yet again changing his mind about the deep-down Jacky character. He felt he would never know the real Jacky, if indeed he existed.

'Ah! Now we have it: Jack's hidden agenda for the new Scotland. Tax everyone he doesn't approve of.

Brilliant, Jack. Show the buggers who is boss. I had better take a quick shiftie before the tariff comes in.' Richard made a show of looking across the bay. 'Ah! Can see the castle clearly now. That view, how much: ten groats?' Richard grew more serious as he downed and twirled the many raindrops off of his umbrella. He was struck by the view, especially the castle. 'Actually, quite impressive... reminiscent of Berchtesgaden.'

'No, Richard. It reminds one of Scotland, actually. Not too disappointing, I hope. And dinnae bother explaining about Hitler's retreat — The Wolf's Lair and all that in up-sky Bavaria.' Jacky delivered this with cold menace. He never failed to be riled further whenever Richard took him on.

He just managed to strangle a sarcastic correcting rejoinder about Jacky's mix up of Hitler's Wolf Lair actually being in Poland and the Berchtesgaden Bavarian retreat actually having the soubriquet of The Eagle's Nest.

'*A bubbling pot of bile and vituperance,*' Richard now decided, his previous ambivalence regarding Jacky receiving a jolt, almost relieving the inchoate concern he had that he himself was being affected by the apparent bipolar Jacky, whose hellish horn of plenty was always ready to spill over.

'And Alex's uncle lives there? In the castle?' Richard's breeding couldn't help disguising his deeper feeling in a tease of the little man.

'No, unless he's the woodchopper or something, ya numpty. I had pointed to the castle because I had moved from the particular to the general.'

'Do you think we could move from the general to the right now; find Alec, bury his uncle and get this last game of golf in?' Brian asked as he rose, his arse cold, sore and tired by the damp sandstone wall he had resignedly returned to. 'Or am I asking too much of such giant intellects?'

'Not the mode I would have employed *vis-à-vis* our goal orientation, but it does possess a certain economy of style. What say you, Jackomo?' Richard laughed, dissembling and feeling guilty at his previous over-harsh, uncharitable thoughts about Jacky.

For once, Brian got in before Jacky; in fact, he was close to interrupting *him* for a change.

'The pubs are open. We go to the nearest wan; we have a pint to replace lost fluids and to fortify our spirits, we ask about recent deaths. Failing that, we get pished, then we visit the undertakers. Or visit the undertakers first and get pished; he's bound to be licensed in this place. An' if that disnae work, we go to the registrar's or whatever you call it.'

'Brian, that is pure dead brilliant!' Richard laughed at his own deliberately awful attempt at a Glasgow accent. His island joy was returning with that oceanic feeling and Jacky's pricks were nothing compared to his hydrophobia — now long behind him. He hoped.

Jacky did not laugh. 'Predictable. But it's worth a try.'

'Whit direction, Jacky boy?' Brian had a hand on his hip.

'That way.' Jacky pointed to the right in the direction of central Brodick. 'Bound to be. Ya nitwits. It's an island. All roads meet… eventually.'

When the three of them were out of sight, Mhairi exited the phone box and made to follow the men at a safe distance into Brodick. Morag took her arm, stopping her.

'Blame the boat trip, Vas, the island air, but… why don't we treat ourselves to a *two-centre* stay?'

'Spell it out, Rag.'

'Always wanted to see what all the fuss is about The Lord Loundesdale Hotel…'

'That wouldn't happen to the nearest one to… what's the course that wee obnoxious one waxed clumsily lyrical about, would it?'

'Ye…s. Shiskine… at Blackwaterfoot.'

'And?' Mhairi teased.

'Well, let's treat today as our day job. Then we'll return here tomorrow for our *night* shift.'

Both women leaned on the esplanade rail, deep in thought, as they looked for a long time at the now fully revealed and splendid glimpse of Brodick castle.

Chapter 14

One armbanded

Brian lay on his back, fully sprawled on the pavement outside the small funeral parlour in main street Brodick. He stirred himself now and then to sup from a beer can from his newly purchased 'carry out'. He was now happier after his exhausting half-mile trek from the ferry terminal: '*Revived*,' he claimed from pavement height.

This island seemed to Richard to indeed have its own licensing laws, or perhaps none, given that it was still nowhere near what passed for normal late-morning opening hours on the mainland. Richard had grim-facedly watched the shoppers step in and out of the next-door mini-market, having to circumnavigate Brian, most with passing 'tuts', a few with knowing and not a few with empathetic, smiles.

Richard, still pretending he was not with Brian, was now simulating taking in the view of a complete Goatfell, the steep, little grey mountain resplendent in a full sun with the contrasting backdrop of tiny white clouds like almost stationary, hovering, non-flying saucers in the imperceptible breeze. He felt as embarrassed as all those other times that came back to line up and taunt and haunt him in times of discomfiture like the present proximity to

Brian, from whom his conscience dictated that he could not simply walk away. (As the temporarily absent Jacky might have put it: 'Dick don't do desertion.')

Richard felt, despite his distinct unease, he could not simply abandon the semi-corpse, could he? Jacky couldn't be any longer inside, surely? Maybe he, Richard, should go in? Richard literally swayed to and fro from one foot to the other as he suddenly thought back to the nearest to a closest friend he once had, assuring Richard that he was 'simply unlucky' all those times that were in the ghostly ghastly persistent queue — caught in mid-masturbation by the pater; stumbling on the mater and pater engrossed in their bizarre and convoluted sexual congress in the study; his sister's fascinating undergarments; the fiasco of the honeymoon...

Jacky crashed out of the funeral parlour door, triumphantly waving a piece of paper and three black armbands.

'Leave it to your Uncle Jacky! Here, put these on. Impress Big Alec. Cheer him up.'

Jacky distributed the armbands. A relieved Richard chuckled and dramatically black-armbanded himself. Jacky took the band back from the hand of a mocking, still prone Brian, and bent to put it over Brian's eyes as a blindfold. Brian left it there for some time.

It seemed to Richard that it helped. Both he and Brian.

'How quaint. And so démodé,' Richard quipped, chirped up again by Jacky's raucous exorcism of that infernal internal queue of ghosts.

'And whit aboot the deceased?' The Lone Ranger asked from the pavement.

'He's past cheering. He won't need wan,' Jacky snorted.

'I think Brian means: *habeas corpus*,' Richard suggested.

'That's Latin, Brian. Aye! Lamlash,' a beaming Jacky shouted.

'So, Jack, it was as easy as you predicted. How could I have ever doubted you?' Richard began to forgive Jacky, but, as ever, Jacky leaped in first.

'*Ego te absolvo*. That's Latin as well, Br…'

But Brian had lifted his still-prone leg in anticipation and pretended to fart.

'I forgive you,' Jacky concluded, as he checked his piece of paper and spoke to Richard: 'Three deaths this week. All in Lamlash.'

'The fresh air, the silence. Fatal combination,' Richard pretended to muse.

'A woman in her nineties — disqualifies her as an uncle. But this one… Are you paying attention, Brian? This is where inspirational genius comes in… It's odds-on this address: *Golf Road*.'

'It does have a certain coarse and, eh, course logic, of course, heh, heh, admittedly, Jack. What is there to lose, but our direction? Which way, Jack?'

'Why couldn't the auld bugger have died on Shiskine? Eh, Brian, make that yer last can, eh? Big match soon. C'mon. On yer feet.'

Chapter 15

Richard's gear

At least it had not rained. The cool stiff breeze that constantly scattered the small leaves underfoot and tried to prise those stubbornly still clinging to the myriad roadside silver birches seemingly remained unappreciated. Especially by Brian.

'New Scotland. Nae taxis: the sheep-dog trials. Nae buses: it's oan strike. Hire a car? Petrol rationing. Need a voucher. Walkin' tae Lamlash! Walking aw the bloody way! *"It's nae distance at aw,"* says Jacky. *"Gives the Lexus time to be repaired,"* says Dicky. Downright liberty, says ah.' Brian puffed all this out through hurting lungs and red cheeks. He was the last of the three to the top of what he prayed was the final brae in this knackering climb.

'Look upon it as an opportunity. It's only three miles, less than one now, and you need the exercise. And shut yer face. Save yer breath for the match. *Partner.*' Jacky tried hard to hide his own breathlessness.

Brian turned at the slowing noise of a car, down the hill behind. As he stuck out his free thumb, the can spilled beer onto the tarmacadam. The car swerved and vroomed up over the hill and far away.

'That's forty knock-backs in an hour. Arran: see it and die.'

'And whose fault is that? Always something in your hand; if it's no' your cock it's a can. It's time somebody got a grip of you.'

'Oh, ah thought that wis your job, Jacky. Your, what you would call, *raison d'être*. Is that French, by the way? And in return for ma sins, ah'm supposed to get your handicap doon tae single figures afore wan o' us dies. Death's beginning to hold certain attractions.'

When Jacky was stuck for a word to – or, more likely, *at* — someone, he quickly found someone else.

Richard's awe was cut short. His wonder was caused by his first glimpse of a beautiful little island to his left — a kind of pocket-sized Arran, a kind of calved offshore offspring, he mused, going by the steep twin peaks that he somehow still managed to look down on courtesy of the gaps provided by the sparser trees at this summit.

'You should take more care driving your motor, Dickhead. Stirling bloody Moss. If Alec had known, he'd have sent a car for us. Stretch limo, it wouldn't surprise me.' Jack suddenly broke off. 'Aw, wid ye luk at that! Ah never get tired o' looking at that. That'll be… That's Holy Isle. Buddhists have taken it over. They charge you for landing on it now; and save your soul for free. Richard Gere was there.'

'Alec's down there this minute,' Brian said almost to himself. 'Signing them up; converting Buddhists tae New Labour. The fats o' the land.'

The combination of the impressive view and the climb being behind them, three slightly happier men almost free-wheeled down the last hill into the little village of Lamlash.

Chapter 16

You can't get the ointment these days

'Haw, wid ye look at that! Ah never get tir...'

'Aye, even you wid get tired looking at that, Jacky. But it would be worth it. That must be the last hole; look, between they two big oaks up to the platform green. Aw, man... bet they'll hire us clubs, Jacky.'

The invisible force that seemed to be drawing Brian and Jacky down towards the finishing hole at Lamlash golf course was abruptly cut off by a demanding *rat a tat tat* as Richard used the huge, heavy, brass knocker on the old Victorian front door of the terraced cottage of 'Golf View'. He applied the extra force he felt was required to gain his companions' attention and return them to their immediate agenda.

An almost sheepish threesome met the wee, very old lady who popped her head out of the door and asked:

'Aye?'

'Eh... is.... We came about... eh.... these...' Jacky pointed to his armbands, strangely lost for words.

'We've goat oor ain, son, thanks aw the same.' The door closed.

'Thought Alec was the only relative?' Brian asked the door.

'The only living one,' Jacky snapped.

'Probably the housekeeper,' Richard said, as he used the knocker again, even louder this time. It was eventually answered and Richard addressed the same little woman.

'We are deeply sorry. Felt compelled to express personally our sympathy. Offer our condolences. Share with you...' Richard began to blush an accompaniment to his flustering, caused by the sudden guilt at how loudly he had rattled the door knocker.

'Tap her for a cup o' sugar and enquire how the Footsie One Hundred's doin' while you're at it. Ask for Alec!' said an impatient Brian to the street, as he was now turned away, lured by Lamlash's eighteenth hole again.

The same old lady peered at each of them in turn. Eventually, she spoke.

'They *are* armbands. It wis yer pullovers... they threw me off a wee bit. You better come away in, then. Foreign, are you? We get a lot of foreigners on Arran. Especially the English. You're no' English, are you?' She peered at Jacky even more closely, eventually giving a horrible, near-toothless grin. 'Naw, you're no' English. Ye can tell. You're fae Ardrossan.' Jacky preened at first, then seemed to Richard to be struck by a bolt of sudden ambivalence.

The old woman led them through the hall, turning to look at Brian. 'He's lookin' awfae green, that wan. He's no' gonnae be sick or anythin'?'

'Get a grip, Brian!' Jacky kept his voice low in the narrow hallway, then spoke normally to the old woman: 'Seasick. Rough passage.'

'You and me both, son. Ah'm sure they watter the *Germolene* these days.'

A few brief moments later the huge oak door was flung open as the three princes emerged running, followed a few seconds later by the now hirpling old woman brandishing a walking stick as bent as her. She shouted after them as she tried to chase them. Richard turned as if to attempt to placate her, but the other two, much more *au fait* with the nuances of Scottish sensitivities regarding senescent grief, hauled him further down the hill towards the sparkling sea just beyond the bend in the road.

The last words heard by the immediate external environs of 'Golf View', Lamlash and the two golfers putting out on the eighteenth green, were:

'Get tae buggery, ya young shitebags!'

'*Now* can ah go home, Jacky?'

and

'Naw!'

Chapter 17

Chauffeur-driven

'Hey, Richard, that's your motor! In't it?' Brian shouted on his return with his 'supplies' to their sea-front bench, then turned and pointed behind him towards the garage next to the licensed grocer in Lamlash's long, narrow, sea-fronted main street.

Richard and Jacky's silent, gloomy contemplation of their further two failures at finding the missing Alec's uncle's funeral in Lamlash was shattered. They turned from their rapidly misting dank sea view: Holy Isle directly opposite was now a shrouding Shangri La. The bit-playing gulls added to the gloom by their sudden mist-muffled relative silence.

'That's all we need,' Jacky snorted. 'That Brodick garage will be busy selling your precious Lexus. Stolen. For *customising* — stretching it into a limo — or mair like squashing it doon and carving it up into two *compacts* or two hundred *Dinky* toys…'

Richard, galvanised, never heard the remainder of Jacky's long fantasy as he ran towards the garage. But he did hear the burst of a beer can and the first line of Brian's rendition of '*It Takes a Worried Man*'.

At least they got a lift back to Brodick, and not only pointed in the right direction for finding Alec and his uncle's funeral, but taken. Nearly. They were halfway, apparently, on what this local had called 'The String Road', having been driven out of Lamlash through Brodick and now heading far too rapidly towards Blackwaterfoot on the western coast of the island.

The young, overalled mechanic was driving the repaired Lexus. Richard, in the front seat, decided it was a fairly decent trade-off for he himself not having to negotiate the countless twists and turns, but he had never been a good passenger in a car, especially in one driven at this speed, with sheer drops down to the tiny sheep and 'wee burns' in the valley through the brown hills on the left and the awesome grey ridge of mountains on the right. Concentrate on the bigger picture, he tried to tell himself, but too often was dragged and shocked back to confronting reality by, if not the sudden swinging of the car, then the not desultory enough observations of Jacky on life, the Universe — but, most of all, the locals. At least Brian was asleep in the back, his head bumping now and then off Jacky's narrow shoulder.

'This takes the biscuit!' Jacky had started again. 'As an Ardrossaner I thought I knew everything there was to ken about Arraners. And this year's Brass Neck of the Year Award goes to… goes to… Whit ye cried, son?'

Richard shut his eyes at the approaching curve and the driver turning his head to answer the infuriating Jacky.

'Wullie.' The teenage, spotty, cocky driver smiled sideways and winked at Richard as he seemed to return to actually looking at the narrow road again.

'Well, Wullie, Richard believes you. Me? Come on, I'm from Ardrossan. I mean…'

'Ah'm tellin' ye. Yer man's here wis the *only wan available.* Aw the hires were oot, the rest doon in bits or up oan the ramp… an' ye don't argue wi' ma gaffer's "Pronto" for a delivery of a spare. So Lamlash here ah came… Well, think yersels lucky… ah jist bashed yer bumper back in and hopped in… Aye, think yersels lucky. It wid huv been the morra afore ye… an anyways, if it wisnae fur me… it seems tae me that the three o' ye wid still be disappearing up yer own jacksies… Who'd huv thocht it… Big Sleekit Sanny.'

As ever, Jacky elaborated, the frustrated teacher in him, plus his raging superiority complex, Richard felt, as he was forced to hear the explanation and the inevitable accusation:

'Sanny is a synonym in this country for Alec, or in your case, Richard, *Alex.* Don't tell me you have forgotten your main client already? — And it looks like *Alex* is even more main than his, or probably *one of,* his accountants has been informed.'

Richard was silent, unresponsive, probably shocked, so Jacky slyly put the boot in — never give a sucker an even break, especially when he is down and you can stand on his nuts.

'Eh, Wullie, ye say Alec, sorry, Big Sleekit Sanny, has some shares in yer Brodick operation: The garage, like?'

'Full partner. Lamlash as weel; and, of course, Blackwaterfit...'

A smiling Wullie got out, stuck his head back in the open window at the driver's side and spoke between Richard and Jacky, and then nodded again towards the back seat at the sprawled, still snoring Brian.

'Amateur drinker, eh? Dinne get lost again noo... hauf a mile up the hill, efter the bend, turn right. Slow, mind. Road's shite.' He faced Richard directly before continuing, his smile now an impertinent beam. 'Oh weel, it's awright for some. Holidays? Golf? Never heard of them. Must toodle. Rush joab. A stoater. Camshaft surgery, ye cannae whack it... Oh aye, eh, Richard, in't it...? Richard, sir, ye'll be gled tae ken, takkin' everythin' intae consideration... nae charge.'

Even Jacky, from Ardrossan or not, had to laugh.

Chapter 18

Would you like to see the body?

Much later, when Richard thought back to this pivotal day, he could still see that sitting room vividly, although initially it was very dim, almost blacked out. To begin with, he could not see any of the detail…

A body lay prominently on a table and a partially built coffin with another body *in situ* was mounted nearby on a trolley. On top of the coffined body were a pier master's cap and a whistle with a lanyard attached. The coffin materials were cheap and indicated that, when finished, the coffin would be, at best, shoddy. Nearby was an old tatty canvas bag with spilled tools, including saw, brace-and-bit, plane and hammer, along with a large tin of creosote with beside it an enormous brush. Wood shavings almost covered the entire large floor space. They had susurrated with every slight human movement.

Jacky's voice would have announced their arrival from outside, accompanied by three sets of feet crunching the gravel path in an assist in its entropic route back to join its fully ground brethren on the western Arran beach less than a mile down the hill…

'This must be it… Look at they divots round there… definitely Alec's.'

'God, yes. Still blocking to the right.' Richard started to worry again about this endemic flaw in his partner's golf game that might one day totally expose Richard's natural inabilities with all ball games, especially a non-reactive, a too-much-time-to-think game like golf.

'C'mon, the door's open. Alec? Alec? Yoo, hoo?' Jacky asked very loudly. Shouting, not whistling in the dark.

'Jack, Jack, perhaps we should wait until... Jack, Brian, I say... respect for the de... Oh well...' Richard's mild protest dissipated in the chill breeze whose ozone was just discernible, as Jacky barged his way into the large isolated cottage.

'What a size!' Jacky exclaimed.

'What valuable porcelain.' Richard paused to gently finger a large vase on a stand in the hallway.

"What a cowp," Brian said, now fully in the main room and kicking at the wood shavings he could just discern on the floor.

'Alex? Are you there, Alex?' Richard whispered.

'What are you whispering for?' Jacky asked.

Brian bumped into and knocked over something that reverberated with a loud metallic clatter, defying and penetrating the cushion of shavings.

'Ssshhh! Ssshhh!' Jack and Richard, for once in unison, admonished Brian.

'There must be a bar surely.' Brian peered in the gloom.

'Ssshhh! Ssshhh!'

Brian found a light switch and clicked it on.

'What are you ssshoossshing for? There's nobody here. There's been nobody in here for years by the look…'

'Apart from him?' Jacky nodded towards the prone body on the table.

'Aaah!' Richard could not strangle a tight little scream.

'Well, he can't hear us. He's deid,' Brian smirked.

'No, son, jeest stiff,' the body said, slowly rising from the waist.

'Aaah/Aaah!' screamed Richard/Jacky, still incongruously united.

They both backed off and stood very close to the coffin, which they had not yet noticed in the dim corner.

The body struggled down from his table top, dislodging a small shower of wood shavings from his ragged, rust-coloured pullover, but leaving plenty still clinging.

'But *he's* deid.' The seemingly very old man indicated the open coffin on the trolley that Richard and Jacky were now leaning against.

'Aaaaah — Aaaaah — Aaaaah!' All three screamed. This was their first united front that day (and would prove almost to be their last).

The old man trundled the trolley with the coffin to the far side of the large room and started to make adjustments to the body. He was presumably an undertaker, Richard figured, and as the trio recovered, each of them warily approached the coffin.

'Look at it this way,' Richard began, nervously laughing, 'by elimination, we appear to have found the correct corpse.'

'*Elimination*!' Brian coughed, spluttered, lit a fag and gave a dry laugh. 'Three deaths in Arran this week and by a process of *elimination* understood only by Jacky, we breenge into two wrong ones before we score. 'First time a ninety-five-year-old widow's told me to get to f...'

Richard cut him off. 'Fine spirit I thought the dear lady showed. And sprightly with it: that last fifty metres was touch and go. Tell me, Jack, how did you know she wouldn't be able to climb the wall?'

Jacky ignored them. He was studying the content of the coffin. 'Dead ringer for Alec: *habeamus corpus*. That's Latin, Brian.' He tapped the bent, busy undertaker on the shoulder to demand: 'Where are the mourners, then?'

'Ye'r here,' came the gruff reply. 'Ah didnae expect ye tae later.'

The trio left the old undertaker fumbling and fiddling, now almost fully in the coffin, and sidled through the wood shavings back to the relative normality of the centre of the room.

Jacky had a smug smirk on his face that he deliberately shared with Brian. Brian just knew it meant 'Told you so!'

'Aye, but it's no' Alec! What good's a deid uncle to us withoot the bereaved nephew?' Brian did not ask.

'Alec'll turn up,' Jacky claimed. 'Has he ever let us down? He's just a busier man these days. And richer...' He appeared to Richard to contemplate this; then, with an obviously enforced brightness, he raised his voice to proclaim, 'So, a wee commercial opportunity has probably arisen and he's chased off after it. All in the spirit of New Labour. But even they've got to bury their dead.'

'Nothin' tae touch the personal touch. That's ma motto,' the undertaker suddenly said through a rough, throaty chuckle.

'Put that in Latin, Jacky. The motto,' Brian said.

'*Nihil tangere...* eh...' Richard pondered aloud for some time as he watched, along with Brian and Jacky, the undertaker take his old canvas bag with the many protruding tools from beneath the trolley that held the coffin. Among another shower of wood shavings, he brandished it at the trio before dropping it. He then took the tin of creosote and the huge brush and wielded them as he began to creosote the coffin.

Richard and his two golf opponents withdrew further as the undertaker spoke over Richard's weak attempts at a Latin translation:

'A smart wee fella he wis tae. Looked just like you.' He pointed his dripping brush at Richard. 'Weer and a shade darker. An' he wore a suit. Clean shoes. We don't get many clean shoes these days. An' he explained tae me that while my profession was the second oldest in Christendom — librarians no' bein' the first, ye ken — that there was whit he called... let me get this right... aye, *economies of scope*. Aw the implements and tools o' my profession could be used for ither matters. Fence buildin'; chalets for the visitors. A chalet is but a coffin wi' a damp course. Ask any faither livin' in wan wi' the wife an weans for a rainy, long two weeks every July during the never-ending Glesca Fair Fortnight. Aye, a great thing the new enterprise culture. A smart wee fella he wis tae. An' it'll get better, he says, wi' the new parliament thingy. Makes yin wonder how we ever managed. Withoot mono-blocking, double-glazing and power hoses. Eh? B&Q. Aye. Keep yer shares in Kingfisher plc if you ask me...'

'Either of you got a clue what he's talking about?' Richard whispered.

Jacky had apparently found a piece of paper on the tall dark sideboard. 'This must be from Alec. Secret government mission. Prepare the natives for the shock of the new. Alec has a facility for exploiting that lacuna between capitalism red-in-tooth-and-claw and incompetent social provision.'

'A New Labour crook,' Brian said.

'*Our* New Labour crook,' Richard corrected.

'What is this?!' Jacky cried. He grinned triumphantly as he read the piece of paper he had found. 'I told ye you can trust Alec. A wee note from him: *To those that may be concerned*...'

'Clichés were never Alex's strength,' his accountant confirmed.

'*Gone Fishing.*'

'Gone fishing! Gone fishing? Whatever can it mean?' Richard's disingenuous question, unlike his last, did not go unanswered.

As Brian scrounged about, opening cabinets and cupboards, no doubt looking for booze — Richard was nearly certain — Jacky over-explained:

'It's where you put a wee hook on a line and... Waken up, Richard: with nine carbon-shafted irons and three metal woods and a putter? It'll be one of Alec's cryptic clues. You know him and his crosswords, conundrums and mystery weekends. He's cooking up something. Independence for Arran? But at a price. *Fishing?* He's cornering the market in diseased salmon. Aims to sell them as a distinctive post-devolution Scotch — correct context, Richard — *Scotch* delicacy. To America or Canada. Something like that. He could even tin them — the wee tins play a tune when you open them with that wee key thing like the sardine tins... *Scotland the Grave...* or *Stop Yer Guddlin', Jock.* The world's full of idiots that would buy that sort of junk, marketed properly. It's scary to think that all devolution might turn out to be is one big re-marketing ploy: *Scotland the Brand.*'

A telephone rang loudly from the hallway. The undertaker, brush still in hand, went and answered it and they listened to him as he bawled only loud '*Ayes*' and '*Naws*' in the background, as if rendering the instrument superfluous.

Richard, despite past painful evidence of defeats, took a deep breath and confronted Jacky.

'There are times, Jack, when the fertility of your imagination is matched only by the viridian ordure that is spattered on the neo-cobbled streets of Milngavie. As Alex's accountant and business confidant, it is most likely that he would tell me of a new venture of the sort. There's more to Alex than dodgy deals.'

'That right? What do you know? You know *dick*. It took a plooky apprentice mechanic to mark your *accountant's* card about Alec's multi-tasking fingers being into the juicy garage Arran pies. No, Richard, Alec just uses you to leak information, to salt the goldmine, to test the water. He uses all of us. And why do we put up with it? Because he can get us on most courses in Scotland without having to cut a hole in the fence. We may disapprove of him in some of his activities, but just as long as he plays fair with us — well, we're all a little guilty of compromising our scruples. Even of complicity.' Jacky turned from Richard to Brian. 'Apathy is still complicity. And so is sloth.'

The undertaker returned to his creosoting amid the stunned silence. Eventually, Brian broke it.

'Jacky, I'm getting quite worried. That's the first speech you've made that I cannae find fault wi'. Can I have a copy? I mean, you actually sounded quite *compos mentis*... Is that Latin by the way? Did you see that, Richard? There was even a touch of self-awareness. Jacky's place in the scheme o' things as plotted by Alec. At last. The truth. He's been using us!' Brian suddenly brightened considerably. 'Great! The Breakthrough. We can still make the last boat.'

Jacky's sullen face confirmed to a partially mollified Richard that Brian's revelatory words had maybe struck home, perhaps even wounding enough for Jacky, deep in himself, to agree.

'Jacky? You're Jacky... right...? That was Alec, he says...' The undertaker looked up, now back at creosote brushing, to see that Jacky was still deep in thought and had not heard him. 'Jacky, that was Alec…'

'What? On the phone?' Jacky tore into the hall. Then strode back in.

'He's hung up! On me. Hung up. Me? That used to do his homework for a fag.'

'You didnae listen,' the undertaker said from the far side of the room as he laid his brush on top of the lid of the now closed tin of creosote. 'He said that. That's what he said.'

'What did he say?!' Jacky nearly screamed.

Richard felt that deep down Jacky's hyper-sensitive pride had received two hard blows in succession.

'That ye never listen,' the undertaker said. 'And Alec says that yer tae make yerselves cosy here and he'll join ye the morn. Or was that the morn's morn? Anyway, I'll be about the business wi' the auld admiral there and you three can aw help oot. In the new dispensation there'll be a cry for men o' many talents. Just like in the Guid Book. Jacky, you've got that look o' the man who hides his glass eye under a lintel, you ken, hidin' yer shite under a bushel. Big Yin, I'll be buggered if ah ken whit use you'll be when the labourers are few and the fat kine are in the haystack.' He turned from Richard to Brian. 'Fetch the bottle, son. Alec said ye were a dab haun' at packin' a glass. It's under the stairs in the wee cupboard. Glesses tae.'

Brian sprang into action and the impressed undertaker looked on as Brian returned and dealt out the whisky generously into four dusty lead crystal glasses. The rumpled old man threw back his drink in one and set about the final dressing of the corpse in the coffin as Brian drank, Jacky sipped and Richard screwed up his face as he sniffed what he was later informed was 'a blend' called *Black Bottle*.

Chapter 19

Carnap city

Richard, despite himself, was watching an obviously bored Jacky, who was messing about with the Admiral's hat and the lanyard with the attached whistle, and who now started plonking his guitar that he had extracted from the boot of the *Lexus*. He then blew the pier master's whistle and plonked the guitar like a drunk Don Partridge impersonating a stoned Bob Dylan.

Richard turned away and began practice swinging the hickory-shafted, rusty niblick iron he had taken down from its place above the empty fireplace. Brian was sitting, sipping happily at the indecent end of the decent blend of *Black Bottle.*

'The auld Admiral in his pier master's uniform, one o' the great sights o' the Clyde,' the undertaker gruffed proudly and loudly over his client in the box. 'Broomielaw tae Gourock, Weymes Bay, Largs, Fairlie, Ardrossan, Brodick, Whiting Bay, Lamlash, Sannox, Lochranza an' here. Wee steamers wi' their own bands. An accordion player. And he never stopped, did he?'

'Relation, was he?' Richard did not ask and deliberately not loudly enough for the old man to hear.

'Fair weather or foul, kept going, same wee silly grin on his big, baw-face, even when the seagulls shat on his heid… and his accordion.'

Jacky started to sing badly with an appropriately untuned guitar and equally awful technique.

'*Wha saw the tattie howkers?*
Wha saw them gang awa?'

The undertaker suddenly joined in with gusto.

'*Wha saw the tattie howkers?*
Sailin' doon The Broomielaw.'

By the start of the second verse, the two of them were engaged in a wee arms-linked dance round the coffin. Brian laughed, but Richard felt he had to take a couple of very unaccustomed and rapid swallows of whisky during this to steady his sensibilities. Then he laughed with incredulity and asked:

'The what? The tattie howkers? I'm sorry, *mais je comprends pas…*'

The undertaker and Jacky parted, bowing to each other, the undertaker returning to the coffin as Jacky answered Richard.

'Typical. Been up here, what?'

'Six years,' Brian wearily answered for Richard, who knew better, despite the unaccustomed rapid effects of the extremely unaccustomed whisky.

'Six years. And you don't know what tattie howkers are! And you standing on the very home of the potato as well…'

Jacky was just beginning, Richard knew with grim empirical certainty, and decided to try and stop the otherwise inevitable didactic flood at source, and quickly stuck a metaphorical finger in the inchoately leaking dyke. He gestured all around the four walls as he quickly tried to intervene:

'Arran. The home of the pot — tattie. Oh, I see. Silly me, I always blamed that abomination on Walter Raleigh. Yet more Scotch myth. Invented by — who will we put this one down to? Sir-Alexander-Fleming-Logie-Baird-Graham-Bell? Or perhaps Wattie McRaleigh, the inventor of the steam-bicycle?

'There's two things that rile me. An Englishman applying the word Scotch to a person. Scotch is a drink — our national spirit — or a native tomato. And that's hit!'

'*Two* things rile you? Come, come, Jack, let's *scotch* this one at birth: you are too modest by half. Why, at least a plethora of sleights, real and imagined, against your wondrous tiny nation have…'

'Oh, to be young and carnaptious!' the undertaker interrupted, shouted over, cackling.

'Car-what?' Richard began, but Jacky's indignant shout swamped his question.

'Me, carnaptious? That's shite!'

An even more gleeful undertaker manically trotted round the finally finished corpse and coffin, shouting at the top of his voice.

'Carnaptious! Carnaptious! It's the genetic memory. The wonky gene. Al Zimmer…'

Richard looked quizzically at Brian.

'Richard, carnaptious is…' Brian began.

100

'What tattie howkers get when an Englishman calls them *Scotch*,' Jacky interrupted. As usual.

A puffing, now stationary, undertaker was back at the head of his coffin. He slid the lid across.

'Leave the lid off, jeest in case the Admiral gets a visitor. Ye never know. Folks wantin' tae mak siccar. See you tomorrow for the interment. Or is it inter*n*ment? Or is that American? Always get them mixed up. I should phone Scottish Enterprise and see if I can claim two grants, and anither yin fae the Tourist Board, Locate In Scotland. Permanent fur wance. The hammer and nails are on the window sill, Jacky, if ye wid oblige in the mornin'. It'll let me get bye wi' creosotin' their new fence up at the Machrie clubhouse. '*À bientôt*,' the old man grinned evilly as he turned back from the hallway to address Brian: 'That's French, son.'

Chapter 20

Miffed and muffed

Richard finished draping the coffin with a frayed, grubby Saltire flag. He studied it, then lifted a vase of dusty, nylon flowers off a nearby cabinet. Two or three rearrangements of the flowers and a couple of re-shuffles of the vase later, he was satisfied with the position of the flowers on top of the coffin's new cover.

Richard was wearing a Paisley-patterned red and green silk dressing gown, a cravat and Italian leather slippers. Jacky, in his original mix-and-match golf gear, sat fiddling with his old battered Spanish guitar. Richard crossed the room and went behind Jacky to start up the huge antique radio on the chest of drawers.

The beeps, burps and farts from Richard's radio tuning must have annoyed Jacky, as he upped his strumming on the out-of-tune guitar as he rose to sing lachrymosely to the flag-draped coffin.

'There's a little box of pine
On the seven twenty-nine
Bringing back a lost sheep
To the fold.'

As a found radio station started to crackle and boom, Jacky broke into a thrash metal version, plus a lousy attempt at Chuck Berry's duck walk.

'There's a valley filled with tears
As the train of sorrow nears
The night is dark
The world is growing cold.'

Richard's strongly disapproving stare was caught by Jacky, who restrained himself and he returned to strumming.

Richard fiddled again with the radio tuner. The static and intermittent voices from the radio got louder.

'What's he trying to get? The old Third programme?' Jacky spoke as if to Brian, but Brian was down the pub – well, the public bar of the local Lord Loundesdale hotel.

'Fascinating, these old valve sets...' Richard said to himself. 'Hear that? That's... that's Germany. Yes, I do believe...'

'English.' Jacky might have been for once wishing Brian was actually here. He probably just imagined it instead and carried on as if he were. 'We've got the log fire, the powdered milk, the stiff Admiral, Noel the Coward fiddling with himself back there... all we need now is the comforting drone of approaching bombers.' He adopted a fair impression (for a Scot) of a Noel Coward accent: *'A good ship is a happy ship. And a happy ship is a good ship. Fire the guns, number one!'*

Richard was too engrossed to appreciate. He spoke again as if to himself: 'Germany. Amazing country for

Kultur. Ninety-six self-financing orchestras... eighty-seven...'

'Marching bands," Jacky said just loud enough to annoy Richard. 'All tuned in to the Lebensraum Polka.'

Richard gave a heart-felt sigh and retuned the radio to find a repeat of the news report on the great debate regarding a Scottish parliament: the one Brian had ordered off on the ferry, the one Richard would have liked to have heard. Even a repeat. But he made the mistake of addressing Jacky just as the Great Debate report began.

'You know, Jack, if I didn't know you better, I would say there was a streak of xenophobia in you.'

'Xenophobia? If you did know me at all, you'd know it was actually *racism.* I hate the Germans because they bombed my Granny... and she never stopped going on about it. I hate the Japanese for no' bombing our factories — just occupying them. I hate the Americans for no' having the guts to nuke the lot while they had the chance. I hate the English for... why do I hate the English? ... oh aye, for ruling, ruining, and stealing what's left. And... who else do I hate...? right! I really hate the Scots for putting up with it. Lord give us Independence, but no' yet. *Because we'll never be ready for it!'*

Richard was allowed less than five seconds of uninterrupted radio before Jacky nuclearly exploded — critical mass arrived.

'Great Debate!' Jacky genuflected, knelt and clasped his hands as if in prayer. 'Oh, please may we have Independence, Lord, but no' just yet!'

'But, Jack, it's what you've always said you wanted. Remember, I was quite moved by the way you put it: that with devolution and then independence you would no longer feel the compulsion to blame me and my tribe for all the biblical plagues we English have brought to your fair land.'

Jacky assumed the tone of a determined and demented primary teacher. 'I bet you voted for this...' he pointed at the radio 'this farce. I knew it.'

Richard, who knew so much better, but could not help himself, laughed out loud. 'But, Jack, Jack, you insisted I vote. That it was my civic duty, that you did not — how did you put it? Yes, that you did not begrudge me a vote, even though I was a bloody carpet-bagging southerner. *Mea culpa, mea maxima culpa.*'

'You know what the Scotland Act will be? A recipe for mediocrity. A charter for arseholes. Every two-bit PR man in for his slice. Every second-rate politician with his hand in the till. Every university and college abandoning engineering and science — the things that made Scotland — for media studies. Every snot-faced English graduate from Saint Andrews working as a poofy *political researcher.* The official result after a stewards' inquiry: we'll be the most governed country ever, but still the biggest apathetic bunch of pusillanimous, otiose toleys. Ach, why bother? We deserve it, whatever form it comes in: the Irish model, the Catalan, Isle o' Man, the Old Dame of Sark. Take your pick and smash the box. The Monkland Model — swimmin' pools for all and jobs for the Tims. The Swiss and The Swizz: funicular railways for the tourists that can't be arsed to walk to the top of the Cairngorms — the smallest mountain range in the world, by the way, but perfectly formed, don't forget.'

'All right, Jack, you're in power, just supposing – no, no, humour me... and this won't go beyond these four crumbling walls... How do you deploy the tanks in George Square? And who is on your list for taking out to be shot?'

Richard, still feeling, and slightly under, the effects of his glass of whisky, started goose-stepping around the coffin, then all of the room, as Jacky fulminated. Richard tried once or twice to get a word in, but failed comprehensively.

Jacky exploded. 'It is *criminal*...! that you get a vote. Six years, and you know what you have voted in? A bunch of Brians! Wasters. You lily-liveried liberal progressive namby-pamby effete English interfering soul-searching do-gooding arrogant ignorant public-school class-conscious deferential ponces. And we are left with The No-Life with Brians. And all in the name, no in *your* name, of *progress*. 1603, 1707, now 1998: another pochle, sorry carve-up — Typical! I even have to translate for the usurpers who have handed it to the no-brainers Brians still seeking revenge for 1690 on an expensively commissioned platter. You and your white-settler colonial condescending guilt-ridden post-Thatcher patronage, and the desperation of hanging on to the rat's end of a lager-louted country that's way past its invade-by date, and seventeen and a half thousand quid for wee cute harmless gormless feckless David Steel's gown — sorry, *robes of office* — still merely a spit in the piss-pot compared to the price we are being asked to pay for their new house of parliament, their inflated salaries and pumped-up egos, their free Edinburgh parking...' Jacky finally ran out of breath.

'Jack, you've got a spot of snot on your cheek.' Richard finally got his word in.

Jacky's rage had made him deaf, apparently. He sighed. 'What's the use of developing a political critique among intellectual pygmies?'

Richard decided he would 'go for gold', as much as anything for revenge for not being able to hear the radio. 'Not sure that one can use that word, Jack, not in the post-devolution cosmopolitan Caledonia envisaged by Ms Wendy Alexander. "Bring me your poor and your persecuted, bring me your pygmies, too." Room for all kinds, Jack, but you and I must learn to call them, not *poor* but "wealth disadvantaged" eh, not *persecuted* but... "aggressively challenged" eh, eh, not... *pygmies*... "height-unfortunated"...'

Richard tailed off and a strained atmosphere was exacerbated by the crackling radio and its 'Great Debate'.

Suddenly, the door burst open. Brian half-entered. It looked to a relieved Richard that Brian was either hiding something behind him or that he was being pushed by someone or something.

Chapter 21

Enter a noble commoner

'Caught you! Damn. Had a bet with the ladies you two would be holding hands.'

Brian was pushed into the main room. Mhairi and Morag were doing the pushing, especially Morag. All three carried bulging carry-outs and deposited them on the saltired coffin. Both the women and, to a lesser extent, Brian were apparently under the influence, but the women strove to maintain dignity, though a fairly drunk Morag had exaggerated difficulty walking with her stookie.

Brian quickly went to the radio and, with an over-the-top face of disgust, switched off the Great Debate. He looked at the two women, registered his horror even further with the radio report and also indicated by an archetypal right-wristed action that Richard and Jacky were a couple of wankers for listening to it.

'Look at the faces, Morag, wid ye. Ye'd think somebody had died.' Mhairi now spoke with an exaggeratedly broad Glasgow accent.

Brian spoke quickly, lest naïve Richard or nasty Jacky spoiled his plans. 'Gentlemen, I present… ta ra… Moreen and Morag.'

'Mhairi and Morag. She's Morag. Tellt yae this wan wis a bampot, Morag.' Mhairi's assumed Glasgow accent was even stronger than her friend's.

'Of course he is, Mary,' Brian winked.

'Mhairi!'

'Just testing. You've passed. Here, Morag, let me help you.'

'Ah'm no' a bluidy cripple. It's only a stookie.' Morag shook off Brian's helping hand.

'It might only be a stookie to you, but to me it's a rather attractive appurtenance. Let me do the honours: see that wee wan ower there — aye, the wee wan that looks really pissed-off — that's Jacky. Our leader. Whereas Richard, the big fella, being a gentleman, is never, but never, pissed-off at anything. Merely miffed. Miffed and no more.'

'Morag, did he say *muffed*?' Mhairi's simulated look of horror more than matched Brian's earlier.

'No, Vary, miffed.' Brian grinned. 'A gentleman can be miffed, but only a lady… yes, only a gentleman can be miffed.'

In the awkward silence, a tentative little knock was heard, then half of a big head of long wavy white and yellow hair came a little into the room.

'*Anyone there, said the traveller, as he knocked on the moonlit door?* What?' The elderly gentleman dressed in 'shabby-genteel rural' tweed and matching scuffed brown brogues fully entered.

Richard's face lit up; he sat up and responded:

'*While his horse in the silence champed the grass of the forest's ferny floor.* Takes me back to…'

Brian, with the slightest of slurs, interrupted Richard's fond reminiscing, speaking to the newcomer:

'Come away in. Garnish the social mix, as Jacky might put it if he wisnae in the huff.'

'How do you do, sir, allow me to…' Richard just refrained from bowing to the white-haired man.

'Oooooh! My, oh my,' Mhairi commented.

'La dee dah,' agreed Morag.

'Nice manners, Morag.'

'Nice hauns, Mhairi.'

'Show's yer bum, Big Boy,' demanded Mhairi, but Richard backed away from the stranger, who politely coughed to Brian, asking to be introduced. But Brian was winking at Jacky regarding the ladies.

'Are they no' class?' Brian's expansive, rhetorical but private question to Jacky was made before over-loudly announcing, 'And from one class act to another, may I introduce to youse, Melvin, fourteenth or something Duke of Arran.'

'Eh, actually it's Neville, eh… and the Seventh… Duke of etcetera…' Neville's slack, pink jowls reddened, complementing his dark purple-streaked nose, all exaggeratedly set off by his snowy white and jonquil cascading waves — the curls almost hiding his frayed checked shirt collar.

'That's it. Duke of etcetera.' Brian quickly took over. 'We brought His Grace for you, Dicky boy. You can both discuss the prospects for tax evasion in the new revolutionary Scotland. Right, Jacky?'

But Jacky sulked in silence. Brian knew he had his work cut out.

'And here wis us thinking the Duke was our chaperonay,' Morag said, then joined Mhairi in a rendition, to the tune and football chant of *Championes.*

'*Chaparones, chaparones ole, ole, ole!*'

Brian spoke to Jacky over the duet. 'Chaparones? That'll be right. Neville promised to let us all see his castle. Brodick castle. Tomorrow night. For an end-of-match celebration. You know, Jacky, after the big game.' Brian was doing his best, as he now addressed the giggling ladies, who had just finished singing. 'Richard's big on castles. He keeps us right on culture, while Jacky looks after our political analysis. And before you say another word, Jacky, here's the programme: tonight, a little social entertaining with the lovely ladies. The morning, we do the decent thing and plant the Admiral and meet up with Alec. And after that: the game. Famous victory on the cards, Jacky. So cheer up. That's the script. Or as you would say — if ye were still talkin' — that's *hit*! For wance we do it *my way*!'

After Brian's rapidly but well-sung burst of the last slow line of Sinatra's self-detested classic (*I did it... my way*), Morag shuddered and spoke.

'Oh, Mhairi, ah jeest love a man bein' forceful. Ma insides turn tae vanilla. Hot molten vanilla.'

111

'Me tae, Morag, 'cept it's mair like yon Baked Nebraska. Yae ever tried it wi' a lager tops? Pure erotic, by the way. Right ero-generous, ah kin tell ye.'

Brian reduced the lights with a leering wink to Jacky, who was equally as unenthused by the prospects offered by the two women as by the drinks Brian passed around. Richard's face betrayed the fact that, for once, he shared Jacky's feelings.

Chapter 22

What fur and plunging hooves

Richard began squatting next to Morag and Mhairi, who were sitting on the couch, arms folded in simulated determined concentration, apparently listening to Richard. Neville was snoring in a corner near the coffin; Jacky was cleaning his clubs lovingly; Brian was finishing off a half bottle of whisky, which he tossed into the coal scuttle by the fire. He was not happy. Despite the drink.

Richard was now fully squatted close to Mhairi and Morag. He spoke with slow control as if to a couple of Martians who had just landed. On the couch.

'No, not at all; it's my fault. Entirely my fault. I'm failing to express myself clearly. Let me try one more time. Communicate, Rick. We three — though there is a fourth, of whom you have not yet had the pleasure — we have this series of matches each year at different venues and...'

'Venues?' Morag interrupted. Ah thought you played golf on a pitch? Naw a stump.'

'Aye, yer right, Morag, sure a venue is where ye keep ostriches. Or a quagmire?'

'Naw, Mhairi, that's a quarantine. It's a stump, ah'm tellin' ye.'

'Ostriches? Quarantine? Stump! Look! It's perfectly simple,' Richard nearly snapped. He stood and grabbed one of Jacky's handy old *Wilson* irons to steady himself as blood fought alcohol for control of his synapses. 'I can't put it any more clearly: each year, myself and Alex — he whom you have not yet met — play ten matches against Brian and Jacky. The winners are…'

'Why fur?'

'I beg your pardon?'

'Why fur?' Morag repeated.

'*Whyfur?*' A perplexed Richard said, then mumbled to himself, '*Whyfur? Whyfur? Whyfur?*'

'Aye, whyfur?' now Mhairi asked.

Richard looked at an enigmatic-looking Jacky, who was definitely relishing this breakdown in intranational communications.

'*Whyfur? Whyfur.*' Richard had now tried several intonations. 'No, don't tell me, Jack. By the process of a critique of pure reasoning, I'm going to get this. *Whyfur. Why fur.*' This last pronunciation was said very softly. 'Ahha! Eureka!' Richard's eye had the gleam of a hyper-homicidal maniac as he stood over the women on the couch. 'Why do we do it? Why fur do we do it? Howfur, whenfur, whichfur, whyfur, catsfur, fake fur. *Tongue* fur! *Whyfur* indeed! We do it because... because... never really thought about it, but I suppose it's a form of male bonding.'

Jacky looked horrified at the very suggestion. Brian could not have cared less at this point, as he sat scunnering further in the hard corner seat.

'Bondage?' Morag struggled upright, as if making to leave. 'Naebody's making me sniff glue lying doon wi' ma arms up ma back. Well, no' withoot ma say-so!'

Brian, spurred to action, chucked his empty can into the bin, stood and blocked the door to the hall.

'Nae bondage, nae tyin' up with or withoot yer say-so. It's no' like that. Here, Jacky, gi'es a laugh, play somethin' on the guitar. There, there, ladies; here, have another wee drink.' Brian went to the diminished carry-outs on the saltired coffin and quickly poured two large vodkas, rapidly adding a little *Coke* to each.

'All a misunderstanding. Jacky, on yae go.' Brian gently forced the drinks on the ladies and Morag back onto the couch.

'No, wait, Brian. There is a serious issue behind that question.' Jacky had two hands on top of his driver, standing like a shepherd using his crook as a prop while surveying his flock, his future and his failed pension. 'Whyfur indeed. I'm beginning to ask that question of myself. The way I see it is that life is a metaphor for golf, and in the New Scotland...'

Brian grabbed the driver and replaced it with the guitar in the hands of a surprised and stumbling Jacky.

'Play!'

Jacky picked at the guitar and tuned it poorly, while the ladies allowed themselves to be slowly mollified by Brian, who had squeezed in between them on the two-seater couch. To the accompaniment of Neville's tasteful and regular but arhythmical snores, Jacky started his introduction.

'This song, probably the greatest of the Depression era, has particular resonance with the parlous state of the present Scottish so-called Economy. Written by...'

He broke off, probably because the two women were chattering loudly back and forth over an increasingly grinning Brian. Jacky listened, now angry and eventually appalled.

'So ah jeest shifted his haun fae in ma leggin's an' ah says, "Etiquette, etiquette, tits first".'

'Here, Mhairi, was he the wan that wis aw spots? Aye. Ah found that a wee bit o' a turn-off maself personally. Not hygienic, if yae ask me. Unless it wis psoriasis, of coorse. An' that dug o' his...'

'Don't talk tae me aboot that dug, Morag. There was somethin' no' right aboot that dug.' Mhairi paused and shuddered dramatically, arms folded under her ample bosom. 'That dug wis a fuckin' *animal*, so it wis.'

'Aye, Morag, even looked like him.'

'Yip Harburg!' Jacky's roar got the attention of the women, who simply simpered and smiled demurely. Jacky strummed his intro and began to sing:

'*They used to tell me I was building a dream...*'

'That's no' a song. A song's got a tune yae can hum. Play's a real song. Somethin' like... Uh... oh, thon wan that goes...' Mhairi hummed something unrecognisable and was joined in her esoteric humming by Morag.

Jacky hurled down the guitar. The loud protesting twang woke Neville.

116

'What? Oh, I never. Well, that time of night. Better check the guard.' The old man began to rise unsteadily from the floor.

Richard gladly sped to his aid. He had been uncomfortable for too long. He took Neville's right elbow to assist the old gentleman.

'Thank you, my boy.' Neville smiled, revealing yellowed dentures to match the streaks in his snowy locks. The top set of false teeth slipped up and down as he spoke:

'Most kind. Now, where was I? Ah, yes. Regimental dinner tomorrow. Nothing stuffy. Come as you are. And do bring the charming ladies. Most gracious. *Tell them I came and no one answered, that I kept my word, he said.*'

Everyone ignored him except Richard as he shuffled to the door to the hall. Neville hesitated and looked at Richard. Neville's face lit up and his top set dropped again as he smiled broadly as Richard began:

'*Ay, they heard his foot upon the stirrup,*
And the sound of iron on stone,
And how the silence surged swiftly backward,
When the plunging hoofs were gone.'

Richard and Neville bowed gracefully to each other, then Neville withdrew as Richard held the door.

'Goodnight, Your Grace.

'Goodnight, one and all,' Neville's voice echoed in the hall.

'Say goodnight, Gracie!' Jacky shouted.

'Goodnight, Gracie.' Neville's voice was more distant, as were the sounds of a violent fall, the possible rending of clothes and a putatively aristocratic fart.

'Beg pardon.' The faraway apology was faint and pitifully delivered.

Brian was busy again at the drinks coffin.

'*Plunging hoofs*, right enough, Mhairi,' Morag stage-whispered.

'Wan less anyway, Morag; bonding, plunging hoofs,' Mhairi said.

Jacky reached Brian at the coffin lid's 'drinks cabinet', his grip on Brian's elbow scaling some vodka in the three glasses framed in a tiny triangle by Brian's large hands.

Richard listened; his discomfort would perhaps be eased by information, but he struggled somewhat with both the low volume of his companions' colloquy and their increasingly pronounced but distorted argot.

'Right, where did you dredge up these two? The wreck o' the *Hesperus*? The raft of the Medusa? And what's this keech, Neville, Duke of Arran and that? Regimental dinner at the Castle! What's going on?'

'Is that no' a member of the aristocracy or what? Met him down at the Loundesdale,' Brian laughed, bent a little to lick a glass and the back of his wetter hand. 'At first I thought the Duke was just a cadger. Tapping drink, you know.'

'Oh, then he must be royalty. Tappin' drink. That makes half o' Paisley cousins o' the Queen. Look, Brian — a brief historical tour of your homeland — this island and its castle were in the hands of the Hamiltons — remember that yin that jumped the dyke for Rhodesia? And now it's the Montroses. Sure, I played golf with the old duchess herself. Well, nearly hit her with a wild shank as she walked her dogs over her links land — but she was ever so gracious about the whole business. Only swore at me twice. Neville's a phoney. Toffs fart, but they never apologise.'

'Hamiltons, Montroses, Arrans — that mob have dozens of names an' aliases. They mean nothing to a republican like myself.' Brian then called to the two women: 'Tell him, ladies: Neville lives in the Castle for… what do you call it?... auld lang syne...?'

'Ah, for Grace and Favour.' Richard was glad of this opportunity to contribute at last. He repeated, louder this time: 'Grace and Favour?'

'Naw! Morag and Mhairi, arsehole!' Mhairi shrieked.

Richard took this with as much dignity as he had left after this long, long day. He was exhausted, not a little intoxicated and totally devoid of *any* further light-hearted *bon mot*s.

'Precisely,' he offered weakly, 'which will also have to double as *le mot juste* and a valedictory prompt… Good evening.'

He bowed and exited with drunken hauteur.

Chapter 23

Pig-ignorant pairs

'Whit the hell was that aw aboot?' Mhairi asked those remaining.

'Basically about misplaced education,' Brian said.

'Well, it'll be the death of conversation as we ken it, but,' Mhairi observed.

'Is he aw there?' Morag asked Brian.

'Richard? Richard's all right. His wife's ran off. But he's still monogamous.'

'Aw, a wanker.' Mhairi took a glug of her vodka.

Morag looked long and pointedly at Jacky. 'Must be the season for them. An' plungin' hoofs…'

There was a long silence.

Brian knew he had little time, but he was feeling confident of success and for once the courage he felt had no connection with the Dutch, whose main outlet for their newly invented gin was encouraging the practice of 'free' rations of their spirit for the troops at the commencement of hostilities, but he felt he might have a battle on his hands, nevertheless, with persuading Jacky to co-operate.

Eventually, after much meaningful staring and heavily pointed leering by the two women and Brian, Jacky, who had pretended to be oblivious, suddenly rose from his chair and headed for the door. Brian quickly headed him off and they started a whispered conversation which the two women strained, but failed, to hear.

'Aw, c'mon, Jacky. Ye cannae just go to bed as well.'

'Want a bet?'

'God, I wish Big Alec was here. He knows the score wi' wimmen. Aw, c'mon, Jacky. I brought the girls back for you... well, and for me, but one o' them needs to be distracted. Look, they're all right. OK, they're no' brilliant intellects, but at least they're presentable. Well, clean. Look at them.'

They both turned to observe the ladies. They, in turn, stared back, until Mhairi slowly cocked one cheek of her backside and ripped off a suspiciously masculine-sounding fart.

'Good arse, Mhairi.'

'You're welcome, Morag.'

Jacky went to leave immediately, but Brian wrapped two arms around him to restrain him.

'Now, now, Jacky, you're just being sexist. It's all right for a man to fart, but no' a lady? Double standards, Jacky, double standards.' Brian, reduced to wheedling, wheedled manfully on: 'Please? To help me out? Pretty please with a *Cadbury's Flake* on top?'

'Will one of them no' take Dick?' Jacky asked too loudly.

'We both will, but no' fur wan packet o'smokey fuckin' bacon between us!' Morag waved their last crisp packet at Jacky.

Jacky tried harder to escape, but Brian was expert in not only the golf grip but also the *Heinlich Manoeuvre*, and held him fast as he whispered desperately in his ear.

'Jacky, Jacky, naw, listen. They've worked all over the island the whole o' the season. They're tired. The season's finished. They're bored. They're game.' He paused and whispered more softly still, 'Look, if it's the stookie that's putting ye off, forget it. You have Mhairi. I'll take Morag, and the stookie.' Brian slowly released Jacky, who now appeared calmed.

'I could try and explain, but it would just bore you, Brian. You wouldn't understand.'

'Kathy? It's her, isn't it? And the weans. Have you no' heard about the death of the family? It's in a' they fancy papers you read. New Scotland. New opportunities. I'm tellin' you, Jacky, once that lot are established in Edinburgh, the fun and games they'll have at your expense. Birds, booze, sleaze, cocaine, free parking in Edinburra, the lot. All I'm saying, Jacky, is you've got a chance to sample what will become the norm for your political masters. A surfeit o' nooky wi' the trimmin's.'

'Listen, Brian.' Jacky spoke slowly, and softly, probably as quietly as he had ever heard him in all their time together, Brian thought. Brian knew this was serious as he looked over again, winking at the women but leaning closer to fully take in Jacky's words.

'Even if I shared your... your preposterous cynicism, Brian, about the shape of the New Scotland, there's a wee problem. Now promise no' tae laugh. I've never told anybody this. Nobody. So, see, if you ever repeat it...'

Jacky breathed in, then suddenly blurted, 'I've never done it with a woman. Just the wife. I don't even think that I could. It's no' guilt or conscience; it's no' fear of the Protestant's final eternal confessional. It's more like... I don't quite know... it just works with her and I... maybe I just don't want to risk failure. You know, catch a dose of sexual neuroses.'

'Aw naw, Jacky,' Brian groaned in deepest despair. 'No' that. What a thing to say to a mate. You shouldn't have mentioned no' being able to do it. It's in ma heid noo. What if ah cannae get the fella up? I'll feel a right dumplin' then.'

'Start off wi' the right dumplin' and see what happens then.'

'That's just cheap and smutty, Jacky, and ill behoves yer role as the moral majority. I'm disappointed in you. You've been a right inspiration: a wee talk on fidelity and impotence; guaranteed to give a man a rager. Family Planning wouldnae dare knock ye back for a joab like all they other...' Brian turned again to smile at the ladies on the couch.

'Heh, youse two! Naebody tell you it's pig-ignorant to whisper?' Morag snarled at them.

'Aye, that's whit youse ur: pig-ignorant, so youse ur!' Mhairi backed up her friend in sentiment and tone, before turning sideways to Morag to over-loudly question her: 'That wee yin, dis he no' remind yae o' Spottie's dug?'

'That'll be the ringworm, darling. They aw look the same wi' that.'

'An' the rabies...'

123

'An' the fleas...'

'That's hit!' Jacky exploded directly at the women.

'An' the violent distemper,' Morag went on.

'That's definitely hit! The French have an expression for words that you wish you had said in a particular situation, but which only come to you later when it is too late to be witty and cutting. This is one of those moments: I will take my leave of youse ladies now; I will go up the stair to my pit, and doubtless come up with a witty, cutting retort that is apposite to you ladies' observation, and I shall say it into my pillow. *Adieu*!'

Jacky exited as grandly as he could manage.

'Awa an' pish ya wank!' Morag had clumped to the door and shouted after Jacky. She slammed the door shut, clumped back, almost completely dislodging the saltire drape on the coffin: as the carry-out was now finished, thus its weight almost incapable of further assistance in keeping the drape in place. She eventually ended the last zag of her returning zig-zag clump and had just collapsed on the couch, causing Mhairi to pop up quite a few inches in the air, when Jacky opened the slammed door, stuck his head in and casually commented on Morag's valedictory shout to him.

'Mixed metaphor.'

He retracted his head rapidly, but closed the door gently.

Brian and the two women stared meaningfully at each other. Eventually, Brian went to the door and turned before leaving.

'Five minutes, ladies. Don't go away. I promise. Back in a jiffy.'

'Must be oan they amphibians, that Jackinoffski,' Mhairi observed, before shouting through the closing door to Brian: 'D'yae want us tae get ready or anythin'?'

Brian stopped in a mid, slow close of the door, breathed deeply and exited hurriedly.

Chapter 24

The dry shot

A minute or so later, Morag watched Mhairi go to the door, open it and listen for a little. As she closed the door and wandered about the large room, Morag reached behind her and took a large book from a shelf and flicked through it. Mhairi went to the far corner to remove a dusty drape from what turned out to be a small piano. She raised the lid and fingered it lightly with her right hand, playing the melody line from *Auld Lang Syne*. She sat on the petite piano stool and turned to Morag, who was in the act of tossing the book aside.

'Well, Rag, had your fun? Can we get back to *our* mission?'

'Not quite. But the language, that has been… quite exhilarating. You know the working class have it all. They can curse and swear properly and no one is surprised.'

'And that fart.' Morag grinned. 'I didn't know a lady could do that.'

'It's been like therapy,' Mhairi said.

'And yet when we get back home, I'll try and say... you know... the F-word. And it'll come out as an incoherent *phucque* or *phaque* or more than likely a mumbled effete *feck*… It's not fair. Just not fair.' She

126

suddenly abandoned her normal speech and resorted to her version of broad Glaswegian: 'So it's no'!'

Taking a felt-tip pen from her handbag, she began to write on her plaster.

'The language thing,' an intrigued Mhairi said. 'Tell me, Rag, you with your literary Masters and such — what I have difficulty with: how does one know when to utilise *youse* and when it should be *youse yins*? Enlighten me, oh Master.'

'Oh, that's non-syntactical, Vas. It's not rule-bound. And yet that's a prime example of Chomsky's syntactic structures. One is born with the inner instinct for language and grammatical structures, and these in turn are conditioned by a genetico-environmental input. In other words, Levi-Strauss notwithstanding, class will out.'

'Oh, Morag hen, you're pure dead clever, so ye ur!' She paused as a thought struck her. 'Here, Rag, just a thought: what is to be our response if your bold Brian Barroo comes storming through that door bollock-naked expecting to impale both of us on his trusty steed? You *have* raised his *expectations*, after all…'

'He's not my Brian, and one does not impale on a steed, trusty or otherwise. Tut fecking tut!' She laughed exaggeratedly wickedly. 'What will I do?' Now, dreamily, she repeated, 'What will I do?' Suddenly, her face was fierce. 'I would like to set him alight! As alight as the ballroom gown I wore when he drunkenly dropped his fag into it.'

Morag adjusted her dress, then lifted her skirt to fix the suspendered black stocking on her uninjured leg. 'Not long after that he was chucked out of uni. Inevitable, given his lack of background. Kilmarnock Academy or some such,' she sighed. 'Still, he did have something. Damned if I can remember what it was. Oh well, *c'est la vie*. Never saw him again, until the ferry this morning. Shocking mess. Here, don't sit there, Vas. Do me a few signatures.' She handed the felt-tip pen to Mhairi as she wistfully spoke. 'I can't believe he doesn't remember. I mean, how many graduation ballgowns can he have set on fire, for Christ's sake? In the post-conflagration, he delivered his immortal male get-out: *"Anyway, I prefer hairies".*' She mimicked Brian perfectly, before laughing mirthlessly again, resorting to her assumed nouveau persona, 'Well, by *FUCK* we'll *continue to* gie him *hairies*!'

'Strange, though, you recognising him almost at once and he doesn't seem to have twigged in the slightest.'

'I was quite plain in those days, while he was rather dishy. Time has been kinder to me, it would appear. Anyway, it was the vomit that confirmed it for me: he did it over my gown that first time. Still, it did quell the smouldering tulle.'

'Give me some names.' Mhairi took the felt-tip pen from her best friend, senior colleague and equal partner in future crime. Now the pen was poised over Morag's plaster. She waited for Morag to speak.

'Oh... let me see... *Noodles* and *Sea-boots*, and *Sixers* and *Bulldog*, and *Hob Nob*...'

'They tripped off your tongue rather easily.'

'*Au contraire*,' Morag contradicted, as Mhairi laughingly finished writing on the grimy white and grey plaster with a final flourish of the pen.

'*Voila*! The cast of thousands!'

They both laughed as the same time as the door opened and Brian came in rather tentatively. He paced up and down, being stared at by the ladies.

'Look, girls, I'm afraid Jacky has definitely joined Richard.'

'An' him married wi' a wife tae. It's this Generation X, Mhairi.'

'Aye, they're aw sniffin' it, Morag.'

'No, Morag, I just meant...' Brian started.

'Mhairi!'

Morag stood and put her arm around a confused Brian.

'Easy done, doll. There, there. Now, that's enough foreplay. Where do you want it? Howsabout that table back there wi' the flag hauf ower it? You could lie back an' think of Scotland dead easy like, whit wi' half the national flag up the cheeks o' yer erse. Ah mean, this wreck of a sofa's already half-done ma back in... Eh, wan condition, by the way. Morag, eh, ah mean Mhairi, gets tae watch. An' oh aye, ye don't mind yer photo bein' taken, ah take it? The Wet Shot, that's aw.' Mhairi pointed to the list of names on Morag's cast. '*They* didnae mind, an' ah've goat tae huv proof for the "*Record*"...'

'An' ah hope that toe-rag of a bluidy paper pays more than the last three times,' Mhairi added, while stifling her glee. Morag also stifled hersand nodded to her co-conspirator her admiration of the role-playing 'impro' and feeling not a little chuffed that their Am-Dram experience was proving more than fruitful.

Brian was horrified and terrified and excited. His excitation almost instantly turned manic as he ripped the saltire drape fully from the coffin, slid the coffin lid aside, reached in and propped up the dead head of the Admiral in a wild try at shocking the ladies, then hopefully steering them nearer the calmer and safer shores of his normal (and prolific) sexual behaviour.

'Noo that's what ah ca' a stiffie, Morag…'

'Widnae count, but: too like Noodles… Mon, Mhairi, doll. Back doon the Loundesdale. We ur pure wastin' oor time in this House of the fucking *Dead.*'

Chapter 25

A lair with a view

The wind on the hilltop felt three times stronger than the stiff breeze they had left down below on Arran's western shore. And considerably colder. Despite the twists and turns of the potholed narrow road, the trio plus the undertaker always seemed to be struggling into the wind's teeth. Even the few, lost, circling, swooping seagulls up here were squawking their harsh complaints: some against the wind, others at the intrusive voices of the four human invaders carrying the coffin.

Richard was tired in body and mind. His determination to grasp why they were *carrying* a heavy coffin was swamped with the ever-rapid panted exchanges among the three Scots in their own language. Something to do with there being no hearse because of a 'hoarse'...

The undertaker took pity on him, Richard felt, more than his golfing opponents and alleged friends, it appeared. Through rattling pants that must have scoured his oesophagus in determined exasperation, he resorted to what Richard felt was the closest the old Arranite could come to performing Received Pronunciation:

'No, son... No hoarse... bugger all tae dae wi' ma genetic chest and throat malignancies... Horse...! Horse die last week... Horse not pull cart no more... Horse "gone" before cart... No horse... no hearse...'

'Watch your feet there, Brian. I'll look after you.' Jacky let go of his corner of the coffin and went to assist Brian, who was slipping back down towards the sea.

The undertaker's translation to Richard was cut short. He gruffed loudly just above the howling wind and through his awful wheezes, 'Naw, Jacky, whit yae daein'? This way, Brian? Noo, Jacky... you're well oot o' order there...'

'Oot ma road...,' Brian puffed and panted. 'Aw naw! Ma best auld Hush Puppies. Christ, they've got queer dugs here: must corn-feed them or somethin'. Never seen wan that size.'

'Baaaah, Brian, baaaahhh! Right, Richard, keep coming as you are, steady, steady, don't breenge in.' Jacky was now a non-hands-on foreman, apparently.

Richard, despite a lifelong abstinence of tobacco, now puffed and panted more than Brian; the weight of the coffin was nearly unbearable.

'Something... not... quite... right... here... Jack. Can't quite put my finger on it.'

The undertaker sounded as if he himself would be his next, immediate customer as he groaned, 'Maybe if oor Jack did put his finger oan it, we'd... Oh, Christ in his pullover... look oot, wid ye...?'

As Brian, then Richard, stumbled and fell, so too did the coffin. Luckily, the second coat of decent creosote just held the thin cheap wood in place, but not quite intact.

Jacky stood back from the accident with his hands on his hips, staring and shaking his head.

'Now see what you've done. Would be better doing it myself.' Jacky looked at a piece of paper in his hand and started to check the lair markers in the small, neat graveyard.

'Come on, this is it here!' He returned to the other three who were recovering atop the coffin. 'On the count of three: three!'

To the grunts from Richard and the garbled curses from Brian, the coffin was struggled back on to their two shoulders. The undertaker gasped and groaned and followed the procession and collapsed once again on the coffin that was now dumped across the waiting battens.

'Jacky, you know how you're always sayin' that everythin' will be different when we get independence?' a partially recovered Brian said. 'Will that include you daein' a haun's turn?' He spun to Richard, who was close to tears and vomit. 'An' before you ask, a haun's turn means…'

Richard just managed to raise his hand to stay Brian, and gasped, 'Pax, Brian, pax. I get the sense of it.'

Jacky, the only man standing, looked down on Brian. 'Didn't want to risk my swing, Brian. With the match coming up. Anyway, I'm the organiser: if it wasn't for me, you wouldn't be here.'

Brian and Richard reflected on this with some restraint for some considerable time, which was still not long enough for the undertaker to fully recover from the steep hill. The wizened old man was gasping and spluttering almost as badly as ever.

'Shame Alex should miss his uncle's funeral.' Richard's voice was just loud enough now to be heard above the howling wind now spattering them with either drizzle or more likely spray from the just-visible sea far below, such was the strength he felt.

'Alec or no Alec, I'm on the tee as soon as we get this where it belongs.' Jacky kicked the coffin gently.

Brian rose, walked a few steps and parked his arse on the nearest headstone — moss-covered and conveniently, if not ergonomically, slanted. He took a lager can from his pocket, opened it and began to drink, staring into the far distance.

The peace and relative tranquillity, despite the vicious wind, was eventually broken by a now-recovered undertaker.

'Ah never had visions o' humpin' the Admiral's box aw the way up the High Hill masel.' The undertaker creaked to his feet. 'Okay, ah wis speakin' metaphorically, since ah'm no' allowed tae hump anythin' or anybody anymair.'

He struggled out something from his trouser pocket. The dirty clay pipe spat out a mouthful of wood shavings on its way to the surface. This he lit with incredible ease, despite the gale. Brian, in admiration, walked over and passed him the can, from which he took three slugs before rifting raspingly in gratitude. 'Peety yer pal Alec could'nae make it; a nice touch it wid have been had he seen his ain uncle awa tae bide awa. Aye, folks are always surprised

134

when they have tae lift the box.' He turned and said pointedly to Jacky, 'That's why I never really dae it myself noo. No' since I witnessed Big Tam Galbraith — he was ma instructor: what an embalmer he wis, put paid tae cremations oan the island single-haunded. Anyway, you could have heard the rupture in Ardrossan when Big Tam tried tae lift Fat Bella Black fur the last time. Bella was the bell o' the kirk, so tae speak; every yin goat tae ring her. Now here ye are...' He bent. 'A rope each. No' you, Brian. Son, you look worse than the Admiral afore ah applied the rouge... How did ye manage withoot spewin'? Dinnae let a burial upset you. Here, whit ye daein'?'

Brian turned away and started dry retching over the low wall of the graveyard, down towards Blackwaterfoot. Richard, as if by magic, produced a Polaroid camera and snapped away.

'For posterity. Nice one, Brian.' Richard grimaced.

'Photographs are extra.' The undertaker gruffed and wheezed. 'Noo, how about a few words for the Admiral?'

'Richard!' Jacky commanded.

'Brian... I...' Richard stuttered.

'What? You and Jacky stuck for a few words? Take a photo o' *that* for posterity.' Brian turned almost grinning as he wiped his chin on his sleeve.

'What I meant to say was... well, we, none of us knew the deceased. Surely it...?' Richard looked at the undertaker.

'Dinnae look at me, son. Unprofessional conduct that wid come under. Conflict o' interests. Unless there wis a wee government subsidy. Could maybe run a module on eulogies. Worth lookin' intae. Aye, an takin' a video while I was digging and eulogisatin'...' the old man continued, his musings now a mumble muffled by the tempest.

'I suppose it would be churlish not to pay some sort of last respects to... but... well, perhaps you could tell us a little about... about the Admiral?' Richard started to ask.

'Naw!' Jacky and Brian roared in near perfect unison, if not harmony.

'Something short,' Richard quickly added. 'Something Alex would know. Would relate to. Something brief. We are in *loco absentis*, after all.'

'That's Latin,' the undertaker said to Brian. 'Let me see. Aye. The Admiral was wee Alec's uncle. Mither's side. Her brither. Or wis it the brither's mither's side?'

Richard had completely lost the family plot. 'I'm sorry?'

'You will be. I am. Shut up. Let The Old Man of the Sea finish so we can.' Brian produced another beer can.

'All right, son.' The undertaker spoke coyly, a smile flickering on his lips. 'Right. Wee Alec and the Admiral. I was there, you ken, eh, know, eh, when wee, eh, little Alec was met by his uncle aff, eh, off the steamer. The Admiral, decked-oot in his number one pier master's uniform, was looking really gallus — that's a hard one... magnificent?... proud...? the ticket...? eh... maybe, eh... resplendent... and gallus is...'

'Usually preceded by *"dead"*.' Brian spoke slowly, his menace manifest. 'As in Dead. Gallows. Tell it quick. Jacky will translate.'

The undertaker knew, just knew, he was but only a short distance from a size ten boot in the old knackers. He decided on a very rapid deadpan delivery:

'Wee Alec, met by the Admiral, the pier master. Wee Alec dead chuffed at important uncle collecting tickets at turnstile. The Admiral punches nephew in stomach, thumps him on back and shouts, *"Who's a pretty boy, then? What'll you be when you grow up, then?"*, and Wee Alec's mammy squawks out the side of her mouth, without moving her lips, *"A sailor, Admiral. A sailor."*

'*"A sailor!"* roars the Admiral. Everybody looks round and the Admiral grabs Wee Alec by the arm and marches him to the end of the pier, right to the edge, points his pier master's baton and barks at his nephew, *"The Sea. The Sea. The Eternal Sea."* And before the wee eight-year-old Alec can even begin to grasp the profundity before him, the Admiral, the auld bastard, pushed him in.'

The wind dropped to a force four, respecting and permitting the relative silence.

'Royal Canadian Air Force technique,' Richard eventually surmised. 'The Admiral was teaching young Alex to swim.' He shuddered at the mental picture, then wondered if it would have worked for him. Too late for that now, he feared.

'Bugger aw o' the kind. Teaching him to drown. He wis famous for it. An' this before there was ony child abuse. But the island overlooked this wee flaw in his character, because he once rowed the Duke's old Labrador across the bay in a force nine, to save its auld paws on the new roads.'

'*Noblesse oblige*,' Richard nodded, his 'watery' discomfort waning.

'French. Right. Fine,' Brian brisked. 'We know all we want to about the Admiral. Let's go. There's a cloud gathering over the first doon at Shiskine and ah want a hit. Wi' all due respect to the Admiral and his nearly departed nephew, Alec. Let's go.'

'Good God, Brian. I know now how you feel, but a hangover is no excuse for barbarity. A modest doxology surely would not be out of place. The Admiral can't have been all bad. Even the Trojans...'

'Stick the Trojans up your... Oh, what's the use? Jacky: if Shiskine's half as good as you said it is, I'm into a practice round. Before... before there's another death.'

'Practice round!' Richard said, and pseudo-mocked, 'Amateur!'

'Jacky, please,' Brian pleaded. 'Say something. Or I am off. You're always on about yer Higher Latin. Mumble something mystical, something — what you would ca' *apposite*. Okay?'

'Ola Kala,' Richard mumbled.

'Whit?' Brian asked, despite himself.

'Ola Kala. It's Greek. It means *all's well,*' Richard expanded.

'OK, OK. Fine. Any language: algebra will do.'

But Jacky had been thinking. 'Eh... *Carpe diem*? *Orate Fratres*? That's Latin. Pray, Brothers. Dear Lord, look...'

'Haud oan there. It's Jacky, isn't it? Well, Jacky, I'm sorry, but that'll no' dae, son. The Admiral held nae belief in a personal God, ye ken. And certainly no yin that spoke Latin.' The undertaker tamped out the used damp shag from his pipe on the coffin lid, his makeshift seat.

'Ah, he was a pantheist. Well, then... May the force that is Nature... take back unto itself... eh...' Richard tailed off.

'I kent fine weel the Admiral wid be a hard yin. Certainly too tough fur somebody fae Jerusalem's Green and Pleasant Land. Nature? The Admiral hated Nature. He'd go aboot spraying weedkiller oan the toon flooers; he wis caught plantin' tatties oan the third green at Machrie — mind ye, that's a' it wis fit fur...'

'That's hit: ah'm off,' Brian announced, and rose from his gravestone.

'I've got it!' Richard cut in fast. 'Look, the Admiral must have believed in something. Everybody believes in something.' He paused and pointedly looked at the undertaker. 'Let's not overlook the psychology of local legends and the embellishments of the indigenous shaman...'

'Well, ah can tell you there was wan thing the Admiral believed in...' The undertaker sucked on his unlit pipe, his sparse hair strands billowing. 'Shoving weans aff the end o' the pier.'

The short silence was quickly broken by Brian starting to laugh. A laugh that owed something to hysteria and perhaps another something to the beginnings of a breakdown. It was powerful and invited participation. Jacky started laughing next, then the undertaker, quickly followed by Richard, who managed somehow to snap with his Polaroid Jacky and Brian laughing wildly.

'Only to catch you two smiling, let it be said.' Richard waved the print dry.

'Well, that's a bugger, so it is.' The undertaker seemed recovered. He was studying the piece of paper Jacky had given him with the grave lair number. He turned it over and over, squinting to read clearly. 'Yae see whit we huv here is lair 169; but whit we should huv is number 691. Ah'm no' blamin' you, Jacky lad, you're new at this an'... Here, whit yaes daein'? Yae cannae...'

As soon as it was clear that a mistake had been made, Jacky and Brian, without a word, sprang into action. Brian lifted the end of the coffin and Jacky kicked the two battens away. Brian launched the coffin into the grave, turned and marched with Jacky out of the graveyard.

Richard started to call them back, then started to placate the nonplussed, spluttering undertaker. He got nowhere in both tasks and began to back out of the graveyard, torn between following the two men now some distance down the hill and staying in the graveyard. His ambivalence was helped by a manic undertaker being apparently oblivious to the recently departed, including Richard, who was happy to watch and listen from a safe distance.

The undertaker stamped up and down on the light brown dirt mound, then calmed suddenly and sat on the next headstone, staring down at the askew coffin. He took out his pipe again and lit it. He stood, wandered a little way, then found the beer can that Brian had uncharacteristically abandoned.

He drank, puffed, then spat into the grave, finally making his peace with the Admiral.

'Wrang grave. Devolution? Recyclical cardboard coffins next. Independence? Away tae buggary. Progress? *Plus ca change...*' he declared to the again-freshening wind, then cackled, 'That's French,' and looked up and directly towards Richard, who turned smartly and ran down the hill.

Chapter 26

Razing the bar

The Loundesdale Hotel's public bar's infamy was deserved. The stories were legion of the manifold cosmopolitan incongruities to be found in this tiny hamlet's only drinking hole. There was a lounge bar, but nobody used it, not even the residents, as it was never open, and residents themselves only ever stayed one night. For many reasons. One of them was the permanent racket from the public bar.

This late Saturday afternoon was no different: drinks orders shouted; jukebox blaring; two harmonicas competed with two guitars, a five-string banjo and four Fair Isle pullovers singing something unintelligible and all drowning out a television with its news of the Great Debate.

The raucous chaos was casually maintained if not monitored by Big Ted, the one official worker, quondam owner, now the full-time barman and still more than passionate gourmand.

Big Ted looked out from behind 'his' bar, over the undertaker slumped on his regular corner stool, to view his packed clientele: uniformed tourists in pairs; holiday-home owners pretending to be yachting types with navy blue epauletted pullovers; kagouled climbers; Fair-Isled husbands and wives; day trippers; geriatric bus party persons. All day they came, and some eventually went. Big Ted checked to see if his sole two residents of last night were still here.

Morag and Mhairi were indeed sitting at the far window table. Then Big Ted's eagle eye noted a tall, skinny Mutt and a wee scruffy Jeff enter his domain. So too did Morag and Mhairi, who gave Richard and Jacky the evil eye with more than enough malice to send them squeezing through the floor's central scrum to a faraway table. The last free one.

'I say, Jack, I do believe those are Brian's fiancées over there. Distinct odour of chip-pan fat,' Richard said, as he eyed the two women, before squatting on one of the last two available tiny rickety and distinctly uncomfortable wooden stools.

Jacky ignored him and began to change into his golf shoes. Jacky was distinctly pissed off. Richard, however, was almost as worried about the golf shoes as the proximity of the ladies, as he fought to the bar and held his own golf shoes up to the one barman.

'All right to wear these in the bar?' Richard shouted above the cacophony all around him.

'Yae can wear stilts for a' ah care. 'S no' ma baur noo!' Big Ted barely looked up from the Guinness font that was playing up and spluttering down yet again.

Richard struggled back, golf shoes in hand, as Big Ted roared after him. Big Ted's roared *bon mots* were one of the chief attractions of the Loundsedale public bar. (The Arran Tourist Board had twice seriously considered utilising these, but at the last minute had taken PC cold feet.) Some of the putative day trippers present were, in fact, permanent residents on the other side of Arran: Big Ted offered good value for their day out. And a Big Ted roar commanded attention and relative silence.

'But nae climbin' on the pool table wi' them on!'

Jacky barely glanced at Richard on his return. Richard started to put on his golf shoes, looking across at Jacky's now-donned pair.

'When in Rome,' he thought, then commented: 'Relaxed on dress code. I like that; I think…' Richard stood and clattered and teetered spikily to the bar.

'I say… excuse me. When you have a moment. It's just a menu I want.'

Richard grew uneasy in the silence that fell. Even the jukebox was silent, the competing musicians had stopped, and now suddenly only the drone of the television's Great Debate had the temerity to attempt to disturb the ominous anticipatory quiet. Richard felt that everyone was looking at him. They were. Now they seemed to be looking at the barman, who seemed oblivious, engaged as he was with a recalcitrant draught stout font.

'A menu? Please?' Richard's voice went from soft to almost a whisper as his throat dried.

'A menu? Bloody tourists,' Big Ted muttered, as he fiddled with the Guinness tap. 'No' see I'm busy? Here!'

A remarkably accurately-thrown tatty menu hit Richard on the side of his head.

The crowd sighed in disappointment, the musicians started up again. Someone put the jukebox into competitive action and declared:

'Rubbish!'

'Big Ted's slippin',' a fat man avowed.

'Gone saft,' someone else agreed.

'Aye, well past his slag-by date,' some inebriated woman slurred.

Richard's *thank you* to the barman was lost in the renewed hubbub as he stooped to pick up the menu and return to sit beside Jacky, who again ignored him.

'Should we order for Brian?'

'Oh, has he started eating now? Did *he* think of *us* when he went off to make up the numbers for the local team? We don't get on the course until three o'clock because there's a team match, and he ends up playing for the locals. From now on it's you and me, Richard. No' Alec. No' Brian. Forget the series. It's consigned to the dustbin of history.' Jacky looked up and addressed the low nicotine-and-cream-and-nicotine ceiling. 'May it micturate down on his bunnet, and may a shag defecate in his golf bag.'

Big Ted, defying his enormous height and girth, went past, rapidly clearing tables of empties. Richard read the menu with difficulty, then gave it to Jacky, who barely glanced at it, before putting it back on the table. Richard picked it up and perused it again. Big Ted, unseen by Richard, came back again and stood looking at Jacky.

'One soup. One roll, please,' Jacky said quietly.

Big Ted nodded, spun round and pushed his way back to the bar.

Richard looked up. 'Was that? Was he? Was that the waiter?' In his panic, he shouted extra loudly: 'Excuse me! I say! Waiter!'

This instantly killed all bar sounds but for the background Great Debate on the television.

'What did you order?' Richard asked Jacky. 'The soup? What is it?'

Jacky shrugged, looking as if he no longer cared about *anything.*

Richard stood, an atavistic sense of self-preservation just stopping him asking the big barman/waiter as he spotted the ladies. They were supping soup.

'I say, girls, the soup. What kind of soup is it?'

'Soup? Soup? It's *fuckin'* soup!' Mhairi screeched through the rising tumult, grumbling further at its vast disappointment in Big Ted.

'Wan, please!' Richard shouted to the barman behind his bar.

'Ye think I am? Uri Geller?' Big Ted demanded. 'So ye've learned the language. So? Wan whit?' Big Ted roared.

'Fuckin' soup!' Mhairi screeched.

The crowd laughed. Big Ted would certainly have been discomfited with this competition from not only *residents*, but *females*, if his Guinness had been flowing properly.

Some considerable time later, Big Ted approached their table with a full tray. He put down two bowls of soup,

146

two rolls, two individual packs of butter and some cutlery, then two large whiskies and two pints of lager.

'Ticky stoffee puddin' or death by chocolate gateau, before yae ask whit's fur efters. There. Two "fuckin' soups". The drams and pints are oan auld Jeffries, the undertaker… Undertaker?' he snorted. 'You've to sign the receipt here an' then present it to your mate Alec. *You* are the purvey.' He left muttering some things about *serving food… selling yer soul for a tourist board crown… and bloody finicky slow-arsed Guinness…*and *chained tae the bastardin' cash nexus at ma age.*

The undertaker was now half-awake, but still fully drunk. He fell off his stool, stood shakily, staggered over towards Morag and Mhairi and began to serenade them to a completely different tune to the three that the competing musicians and the juke box were now playing. His sashay towards the women was stopped short as he was hooked by Big Ted, who returned auld Jeffries to his allotted seat at the corner of the bar.

Somehow, the old man spotted Jack and Richard across the crowded room. 'Ahwidjineyeboysbutahmthatfu'ahcannaestaunawrabest!' he cried, lifting his empty glass in toast.

'No, Jack, I won't ask you to translate; I'm beginning to learn the language, and that was all about *mair drink*. I will now say Grace: Lord… No more alcohol until Christmas. Please.'

Jacky raised his glass towards the undertaker.

'Sláinthe!' he replied, then looked to Richard to explain. 'That's Gaelic.'

The undertaker sneaked shakily off his stool and swayed towards the women again to begin a simply awful rendition of '*She Wears My Ring*', but was pretty smartly stopped by a well-aimed stookied leg to the shins and a warning from the wearer:

'Wear your ring? Ah'll kick it bloody in fur ye.'

At that, the whole golf team arrived, singing. Brian was borne shoulder high.

We are the champions. We are the champions. They were all singing except Brian.

A small grey golfer in an over-long, bright heliotrope pullover shouted, 'Big Ted! Give this man here…' — Brian was lowered and clapped on the back — 'whatever he wants!' The little golfer turned and boomed to the whole bar: 'Three and a half; two and a half! Machrie well and truly stuffed! At!… Last!'

The team, apart from Brian, started chanting again: '*Championes, Championes…*'

'Hey, youse! That's oor song! An whit's that bam daein' wi' the Loundesdale team?' Mhairi's question was left hanging in the golf mass now elbowing its way through to the bar.

Some time later, Big Ted arrived beside Jacky and Richard. He lifted the two full drinks from his tray of empties. He placed a pint of lager before Jacky. 'The pink gin's for you, petal,' he said to Richard. 'Frae Brian, the hero of the hour, ower there.'

Brian, now sitting high on the bar counter, saluted Richard and Jacky over the sea of heads with his own whisky. Jacky ignored him, while Richard made a salutary, conciliatory gesture with his strong gin and weak smile.

For one of a few times that afternoon, there was a momentary lull in the racket in the bar. The Great Debate on the small television high up on the bar wall could actually be heard.

'Hey, Ted!' Brian bawled over everyone. 'All right if we have the telly off? Bloody politics! Makes me sick!'

Big Ted had to consider his residents. It was in his contract and he was on his final warning from the wee sleekit bastard he had lost his bar to in a drunken golf bet.

'Ladies, do youse two mind if I switch the telly aff?'

Morag pointed at Brian and shouted at Ted: 'Fur aw we care, ye can shove it up his shiter!'

'That's Scottish, by the way!' Mhairi stood and screeched at Jacky, then sat and spoke loudly to her friend: 'There, Morag ah've done it again. An' ah swore ah widnae swear; it's seein' they creeps frae the House o' the Dead that did it.'

'Bunch o' creeps!' Morag struggled up to shout over to Jacky and Richard.

'Hey, Brian, ye're in there.' Big Ted nodded towards Morag. He was back behind his bar, remote in hand, as he switched off the television. 'Nae cunt's interested in this shite anyway.'

'Hey, you two. Enjoyin' yourselves?' Brian stood over his two mates. 'Listen, ah'll see you the night at the castle. Neville's laying on some sort o'... whit did he ca' it? Anyway, it's a swally.'

'Soirée, Brian.' Richard was slightly perked up instantly, despite being sleepily intoxicated. 'Neville's having a *Soirée*. It's French.'

'Naw, Richard. A *swally*. It's Glesga. By the way,' Brian said.

'Hey, Brian! Chop-chop! Game on!' Big Ted shouted over.

'Better go — they want me tae teach them pool noo. See you the night, then…'

Richard giggled and finished his gin. 'A ce swalley.'

'*That's* French, Jacky,' Brian said, as he moved away, but then stopped and turned back. 'Oh, by the way, ah saw Alec.'

'Alec? Alec who?' Jacky pretended to ask. 'Oh, Alec that used to be our golf mate and whose uncle we just happened to bury the day? That Alec. You saw him, then? Where? What did he say? Did he mention his mates? Did he...? What did he say?'

'Oh, ah wisnae speakin' tae him; he was six holes ahead, wi' some crowd o' green wellies fae Dougalston Estate. Upper class timeshare mob: shootin', fishin', fornicatin', somethin' like that. It was Alec awright; could tell that swing a mile away…'

'Blocking to the right.' The three of them spoke as one.

'He was away when ah finished the match; but the auld undertaker's assistant is goin' up tae Dougalston tae mend a fence or embalm a ram or somethin', an' he'll tell Alec to be at the Castle the night. Then we can have the decider in the morning.'

150

One or two in the small crowd around the pool table shouted impatiently that it was Brian's turn to play. Brian apologetically shrugged his shoulders to his two companions, turned and left them.

Richard smiled, his eyes almost watering, as he spoke to an even more sullen Jacky. 'Well, well, good old Alex. He always turns up trumps in the end. I'm beginning to get a good feeling at last about this little adventure, Jack. You know, I've felt somewhat incomplete since I came to Arran. I think all will be well again when we four are once more enjoined in battle. What say you?'

Big Ted appeared alongside with the undertaker gripped by the collar as he steered him to the front door. The undertaker looked at Jacky and Richard and called out like WC Fields: 'Throw the bums out!'

And Big Ted threw the bum out.

Chapter 27

The stars at night

Richard and Jacky were asleep and snoring. The bar, although still busy, was less noisy. Big Ted and Mhairi had just lost to Brian and Morag at pool and were grudgingly paying up.

Brian felt that a tepid warmth had crept into the relationship with the women that may well have been a little more than drink-related. The two women went to resume their seats. Big Ted went behind his bar. Brian hesitated, then went to the jukebox and eventually inserted a coin.

As Owen Bradley and his Quintet commenced their version of '*Blues Stay Away From Me*', he strode, hand out, to ask Morag to accompany him. With withering contempt, she lifted her stookied leg and shook it at him. Before Brian could turn away, Mhairi stood and took Brian's lowering hand.

Over Mhairi's shoulder, Brian took not a little satisfaction as he took in a pig-sick Morag becoming much sicker than a sow with diverticulosis as she watched Brian and Mhairi get ever closer in their dance eventually assuming the archetypal bum-grabbing hold. Towards the end of the song, they ever more heartily joined in the words, ending in a fully-fledged duet. When the music died, Brian went to escort Mhairi back to Morag, but thought better of it and went to the bar instead.

'If you stopped playin' with women, Brian, you could make a livin', at pool.' Big Ted handed Brian a Guinness that had finally flowed perfectly.

'Got a rival offer, Ted. From Germany. Seems two-handicappers can have a half-life teaching in the Fatherland. Golf's still in its infancy uber alles.'

'Scotland on the verge o' great things tae? Be a mug no' tae go tae Germany.'

'Ah think so. Aye, probably.' Brian looked over to the sleeping and snoring Jacky and Richard. 'Nothin' tae keep me here,' Brian said sadly, turning to lean his back against the bar. Supping the dark cream froth, he looked over towards the two women who were out of his earshot, but both were openly looking at him. Whispering for once.

'Yes, I detect a certain *je ne sais quoi*... oh, call it brute magnetism there. Pity he reeks of cheap alcohol and even cheaper nicotine from every pore. Still, I'm sure you could do something in that direction if you had a will to... Rag?'

'Do I really want to, Vas, I ask myself? Why haunt the past when the present is just as grey. No! Let's continue to have our little amusement. Not forgetting our main one, *ce soir*. We can regale the staffroom with *le petit* in the bleak mid-winter. Men really are such shits.' Morag had swivelled to look at the snoring Jacky and Richard. 'I mean, just look at those two morons. You could do anything to them and they wouldn't know. I could so easily kick that wee one...'

Brian and Big Ted, who had been looking at the ladies all the while, now turned their heads to follow the gaze of the women towards the two sleepers, each now snoring louder.

'They'll begetting ma place a good name,' Big Ted said.

Brian laughed and went over to Jacky and Richard and roughly prodded them both.

'Heh, you two, still enjoyin' yourselves?!' Brian roared in Jacky's ear.

Jacky jolted upright.

'Whit? What time is it?!' Jacky looked at his watch. 'Oh, merde! We were on the tee two hours ago. Double merde!' He jumped up, grabbing Richard. 'Come on, ya dick, we've still got time!'

He shook Richard violently to fully waken him, before running towards the door; but he stopped short and rushed back to pick up his clubs from under the table.

The whole bar was laughing.

'Move it, Richard! We've still got time... we've still got time... we've still got time!' he pushed a sleepy Richard towards the door.

'Ye huvnae, Jacky!' Brian was the only one left in the bar who looked less than happy. But his words went unheard.

Jacky and Richard stood on the front steps of the hotel. Richard was peering up into the blackness that would have been complete but for the occasional desultory twinkle. He pointed up to ask: 'Isn't that Sirius B? What do you think, Jack? Just about playable?'

Chapter 28

Well met by moonlight

'*Ça suffit*, Rag.' Mhairi carefully closed the flap on the full rucksack.

'Job well done, Vas. Well done.' Morag switched off the torch.

The hunter's moon took over lighting this small walled section of the gardens of Brodick Castle. An indeterminate animal gave a light wail in the nearest copse.

Mhairi bent and placed both hands around the rucksack, grunted as she slowly lifted it.

'You certain you'll manage it, Vas?' Morag silently cursed her incapacitating plaster.

'With a couple of stops for recovery, maybe. It can't be but half a mile to the digs. Let's go, partner, I'll be fine. All downhill.' She hoisted the rucksack onto her back, the weight causing her to take two quick backward steps to avoid overbalancing.

They had left the other side of the island and the raucous Loundsedale bar some two hours ago. The taxi had dropped them off at the nearest boarding house to the castle that was still functioning in October. Now their objective had been achieved, they started to make their way down the slight incline leading back to the main road and the small cottage where they would spend the remainder of their last night on Arran. Their last night ever on Arran they were certain

The moon did its job: the torch was not needed.

But suddenly, another torchlight beam swung and swayed towards them. Mhairi was caught in its beam in the act of lowering the rucksack that she quickly tried to push into the nearest thick bush.

'Haw. There they are! Where ye been? We've missed youse ladies. Jacky here said that that wis the last we wid see of youse two. What dis he know? Here, let me help you wi' that. Now that is what ah ca' a carry-oot! Look at this, Neville…'

'Most gracious, Brian. Most gracious.'

Chapter 29

Get it right down ye

It was, in fundamental respects, a 'candlelit dinner'. There were candles and there was food and it was late enough (and, being Arran, drink, naturally — wine, spirits, beer and Irn Bru). The long dining room of Brodick Castle was covered in lit candles. The almost as long dining table had a spread of scattered 'suppers' in newspaper wrappings — fish, pie, sausage, hamburger and haggis; the full silver service with redundant silver cloches incongruous and unsullied; only the fine crystal goblets were in use.

All eight sat, ate a little, except Big Ted, who ate constantly, and drank a lot. (Except Big Ted, who had not touched a drop since losing his bar in that drunken bet.) Neville presided at the head of the table. Richard, Jacky, and Brian were on his right, in that order. Opposite them on Neville's left was Mhairi, Morag, the undertaker and Big Ted (the only one sober and who drove them west to east in the hotel minibus for Neville's promised 'near-midnight feast'. Big Ted, in a spirit of crazy adventure and abandon and experiment and romance, and in pursuit of free non-Lounsedale decent food and some fun for a change, had left the Lounsedale public bar in the charge of an Honesty Box until he got back, having locked the one pub exit door — after he had marked all the decent spirit bottles.

Mhairi and Morag shuffled in their seats. They looked strangely nervous. Mhairi bent to look under the table at their large rucksack that she had just kept from Brian's big, eager paws as she and Morag had been escorted to Neville's 'secret entrance' into the castle (aka 'the back door').

Morag raised an eyebrow in query regarding the rucksack. Mhairi nodded affirmatively and smiled quickly as she pretended not to listen to that wee pompous loud squirt opposite.

'What was that famous line of yours? *I'm beginning to get a good feeling about this little adventure, Jack?*' Jacky sarcastically addressed Richard, but Brian responded instead.

'And here, Jacky, it could get better yet,' Brian whispered, 'much better.' He indicated the two women, who were looking at him in what Brian took to be nervous anticipation of a sexual nature. 'The ladies over there, we've done them an injustice. They're actually quite, well, nice when you get to know them. They're prepared to overlook that little misunderstanding back at the Admiral's. The thing is, they have a problem and we can maybe help them out. You see, Jacky, they were part o' a troupe o' lap-dancers run by Alec and...'

'Arran? Lap-dancers? With a stookie? And for an encore she kicks your head in? Lap-dancers?' Jacky had caught some of Brian's whispering tact, but now he erupted and bawled directly at the two women opposite.

158

'What's the capital o' Finland?' He was met with two blank and now fierce female faces. He turned again to Brian. 'See!' Now he turned on Richard. 'And, of course, you, as Alec's accountant, knew about this little sally into immoral earning!'

'Jacky, you're being very unfair on the ladies,' Brian whispered, desperately trying not to raise his voice, despite wanting to thump Jacky, and not for the first time since sailing. 'Only in your mind would you make the association of dancing with prurience. Yeah, ah know, ah know, ah can talk that way as well as you two; ah wis at uni wance. Yeah, ah know... what a day that wis.'

Jacky had not been listening, as usual. What was unusual was his soul-searching: *Am I really like that, always thinking the worst of people?* he asked himself. He looked directly across the table to the strangely quiet women. *You know, Brian's probably right; I've judged those girls by their appearance. No! By their accent, by the way they mangle the language. By their vulgarity, their coarseness. He's right: I've become sour and cynical. That's no' me. Deep down that's no' me. Right, that's hit!* Jacky turned sideways to Brian, now whispering with a strangely serene smile on his usually 'torn' face: 'OK, let's hear about the ladies' problems and how we can help out.'

Brian could not believe his luck. 'Well, it's an affair of the heart, sort of. You see, Morag an' me... naw, Mhairi ...an'... Here, which wan's got the stookie? Aye, it's Morag. Well, her an' I are terribly drawn to each other and...' Brian faltered, being much more at home with the

159

actions of love than the unaccustomed male-mainly hypocritical verbiage of romance.

'You've had a good bucket, made new pals. Got a round a golf in. Became a local hero for saving the pub in a play-off. May as well get your hole as well. It always comes down to that,' Jacky sneered.

'Jack, Jack. Language.' Richard nodded towards an oblivious Neville, who was tucking into a fish supper with gusto. 'We have company. And... of course, the ladies.'

Brian ignored Richard's plea as he continued whispering to Jacky. 'It's no' quite as simple as that. They are a pair. If Mhairi disnae get fixed up, then Morag does not come across. You see, Mhairi really respects you and...'

'Well, do without like the rest of us,' Jacky said, and looked up to catch the cynicism on Brian's face. 'I know. I know. If you go without for a couple of days you get a rash and that big horrible plook that I can't stand breaks out on your nose.' Jacky paused, thinking. 'I don't suppose a wank would do?'

'No' really, Jacky. But thanks for the offer,' Brian replied, before rapidly hurrying on: 'Mhar, eh Mor, well wan... she really does like you. Ah heard her say as much when you were sleeping back at the pub. Now how did she put it? Aye, how vulnerable you looked. That's what she said.'

'*Vulnerable*? Me? She said that about me? Well now. That's, you know, pretty perceptive. For some reason people that don't know me think I lean... tend towards the brash side. *Vulnerable*? That woman, that lady, is a canny student of human nature. But I told you once before… in total secrecy… here! Maybe it's something I should be proud of, though…' He lowered his voice further to Brian. 'I'll no' be able to do it with another woman. I just know it.'

Brian, seeing Jacky was wavering, had been encouraging Mhairi to make a move by secretly signalling to her with his head

Mhairi knew what Brian wanted. He wanted Morag. That was obvious. Morag wanted Brian, and that was even more obvious. But Mhairi wanted sex. Celebratory sex. A quick, raw, unadulterated, unembellished *shag*. It had been ages… far too long. This wee squirt would do. Any squirt in a… He might even be good. If she could shut him up. She would shut him up. *Nae bother.*

She got up and began to sing to Jacky, accompanied by Brian on the guitar he had quickly picked up.

'There's nought but care on every han',
In every hour that passes, oh.
What signifies the life o' man,
An' 't were na for the lasses, oh.
Green grow the rashes, oh;
Green grow the rashes, oh;
The sweetest hours that e'er I spent,
Are spent amang the lasses, oh.'

As she finished her song, she held out her hand to Jacky, who went towards her as if hypnotised, perhaps traumatised. He took her hand and was drawn out of the room.

Brian raised his glass towards Morag, who responded with a smile full of promise.

Richard and the rest all fell cheerily to eating and drinking again. (Except Big Ted, who had never stopped eating and who never drank alcohol, but he could eat for Scotland, provided it was food not contaminated by Chic the clarty Lounsedale chef — oh, Big Ted could tell some tales about Chic 'Clarty' McCartney , and sometimes did when food orders in the bar became intolerable in volume.)

Richard was… tipsy…? merry…? drunk? Who cares? he thought, and laughed openly, freely. He was happy. Truly happy for the first time in goodness knows how long. And it had nothing to do with the game of golf and the match, the series that he thought had provided what had previously passed for occasional contentment, a relief, certainly nothing compared to this. This happiness. He was truly happy for the only time, perhaps since long before coming to this previously alien country… He must find out more about this intriguing noble old chap on his left — he felt it only polite, a kind of 'non-*noblesse oblige*', he chuckled silently, in place of common politeness and courtesy to one's host.

'I say, Your Grace…'

'Neville, please. Neville, old man. Informality — let it be tonight's watchword.'

Richard entered the new land of Euphoria.

Not too much later, but too, too soon for Richard, Jacky burst in bursting with good cheer. He exchanged a couple of knowing winks with Brian, who made one with

Morag, then stood and suggested she did the same, as it was now time for the two of *them* to 'retire'.

'There you are, it's your Uncle Jacky. Remember I said I'd never be able to do it with another woman? 'Member? Right again. I couldnae!'

Brian collapsed into his seat and then sat with his hands over his head, muttering, as Mhairi entered dramatically, pointedly adjusting herself, then primping her hair with both hands

'Right hen, that's it! We're offski oot a here, Morag! Never been so mortified in a' ma nelly.' She went up close to Jacky. 'If ah wisnae such a lady, ah'd tell you tae go an' fuck yerself! But whit would be the point?' She swivelled to Brian. 'An' as fur you! Call yourself a pimp?' She impressively reverse-swivelled (an impressive *fleckle*, even) to face Morag. 'Come on, doll, we'll try the seamen's mission.'

Morag made to pick up their rucksack from under the table, but Mhairi's quick, surreptitious but severe look made her leave it.

No one else noticed, except Richard.

Morag clumped to her foot and turned to Big Ted, who had been concentrating as ever on eating.

'Hey, you! You comin' or whit? There's anither two pudden suppers in it fur ye.'

Big Ted crammed some more lukewarm chips into his mouth, rose, quickly collected a couple of sausages in one huge hand, and with the least hint of a nodded apology towards Brian, left. The ladies had already exited with extreme hauteur, despite Mhairi's frantic hurrying of the clumping Morag.

'An', eh, they ca' yae Big Ted. Why fur?' Mhairi's question echoed from the hall.

Jacky cheerfully resumed his seat just as the undertaker revived briefly from his drunken slumber.

'Hey, smiler! Aye you, ya nyaff! Gie's a song!' he loudly demanded of Jacky.

Big Ted came back in and hooked the undertaker under the arm. 'Naw, don't thank me,' Big Ted said to Jacky, as he dragged the undertaker out of the room. 'Efter a', it's ma *raison d'être...*' He stopped at the door to add towards Brian, 'That's shite, by the way', then left in pursuit of his two hot puddings.

Chapter 30

Rare species

Brian was meditating on events as Richard revealed that the ladies had left their rucksack. He tried to lift it, then gestured its existence to Jacky.

'The ladies seem to have left their make-up bag. Think I should go after them, Jack?'

'Forget it. They'll come back in the morning, all sheepish and apologetic.' Jacky bent to the rucksack with one hand and failed to lift it. 'What's in here? Three sand and one finest blue *Portland* for their makeovers?' Jacky began to pull the rucksack open, but Richard stayed his hands.

'Sorry, Jack, but some things are just not done.' He pushed the rucksack against the table leg, mumbling, 'Not even to those harridans.'

Brian spoke in a very controlled voice. 'Jacky, would it be unfair if ah wis tae say that ye're heart wis never really in this? Ah mean the ladies, the... the... you ken, the... well, this wee swally? In a sense, this wis aw in your honour. My gift to you. Ah'm ah bein' unfair?'

'Brian, you know me: never one to complain; but I mean to say, for instance, the ladies — lap-dancers? Neville here? Earl of Arran?' Jacky did not bother to acknowledge Neville, whose head was now fully engaged with some newspaper-wrapped food. Jacky went on to ask, 'Would Big Ted no' have known him?'

'Big Ted's a *local*! You don't think the Duke would talk tae a local, dae ye?' Brian turned to Neville who was oblivious as ever at the head of the table, his head now fully into his fish supper. He could have been asleep — and could have been for a little time. Brian nodded to Richard. 'An' Jack the lad here is supposed to be a socialist?'

'All I'm sayin' is: If he's the Duke of, why use the secret back door?'

'Seen the size of the front door? The key would give you a hernia.'

'Difficult for the duchess to secrete it under the door mat, eh?' Richard giggled, then examined the plate he had finished eating from, turning it to reveal its hallmark, then addressing a now uprighting Neville: 'I say, this is rather priceless…'

Neville's head rose a little further. It nodded slowly. He may simply still have been asleep.

'They are all bloody nuts, the aristocracy. You should know that, Jacky. You told me it comes from humpin' the servants and dodging the debt collectors; or vice versa come to think of it as that is how they apparently like it best… anyway, part of the castle's closed off, Neville says. National Trust and that. For renovation. Probably explains the candles. Anyway, have we got a choice? Where else do you suggest? Another night in the Admiral's haunted dockyard? And, well, the hotels... you being poor, ah thought you would have jumped at this freebie.'

'Right, right. Okay. Okay. But where's Alec? If I don't get a game in, I'll need to lie to Kathy about the golf at least when ah get home. I've got to get a game in. Okay? And by the way, we're no' poor. Just uncomfortable.'

'He's comin', Alec's comin'. Ah sent a message to him. Okay?'

'Ola kola. Ola kola. Simply a wonderful experience...' Richard persisted in speaking to the Duke. Who might have been awake… as he spoke:

'Hoped you'd care for it… Richard, isn't it…? And these…' Neville gestured to the food in the newspapers on the table in front of him. 'Wonderful. And the name: *fish supper*? Really…?' Then he suddenly started to sing in a surprisingly pure though reedy voice:

'Underneath the water weeds
Small and black, I wriggle,
And life is most surprising!
Wiggle! Waggle! Wiggle!
There's every now and then a most
Exciting change in me,
I wonder, wiggle! waggle!
What I shall turn out to be?
"The Tadpole", by E Gould.'

'What's he on about now?' Jacky asked Richard. 'What was that he said in the bushes on the way up? Aye… something about…' — he now badly mimicked Neville — '*the beech tree track*.'

167

'*Path*, Jack, *The Beechwood Path*,' Richard corrected, then recited through only a minor slur:

'*In autumn down the beechwood path*
The leaves lie thick upon the ground.
It's there I love to kick my way
And hear their crisp and crashing sound.

J Reeves, "*Beech Leaves*". Poetry, Jack: His Grace is cultured. Don't suppose you covered that stuff at the old Strathgorbals tech. More along the lines of:

To the woods, young man
Bring a woman if you can
And if you can't bring a woman
Bring a hairy-arsed man.

'*Old tin can*, tut tut, Richard,' Brian mock-corrected, then bawled:

'*There was a young girl called Alice*
Who shat in the Vatican Palace
What led to this deed
Was not physical need
But pure fucking Protestant malice!

Anon. Or maybe Torquemada…'

'Another Winchester man!' Neville clapped his hands, his weather-worn face now a red beacon of delight. Beaming avuncularly, he launched into:

'*There was a young man from Bengal*
Who had a hexagonal ball
The molecular weight
Of his penis times eight
Was twice the square root of fuck all.

Me. Good show.' Neville recovered his breath. 'Goodness. This has been fun. Takes me back to the war. He took a deep lungful of chip-fatted air and began to recite:

'On linden when the sun was low
all bloodless lay the untrodden snow
and...'

A newspaper-wrapped food package, chucked by Brian, stopped Neville's recital as it landed on his empty plate.

'Have another fish supper, Your Grace, and give your tongue a treat.'

'Your Grace, could I trouble you to ring for some salt?' Richard asked.

'And some brown sauce,' Jacky added sarcastically. Jacky was particular about his food. Even cold chips. Or, perhaps, especially.

'And a penny pickle.' Brian was not into food and it was never into him for long.

'Tiny problem there,' Neville apologised. 'Given the servants home leave — end of a hard season and all that:

Something told the wild geese
It was time to go,
Though the fields lay golden
Something whispered "Snow!"
Something told the wild geese.

R Field. I'm nearly sure... and, quite frankly, silly really, I suppose, but I just don't have a clue where they keep things. Like MFI, we run the show on a strictly need-to-know basis.'

169

'Is it the same with the electricity?' Jacky rose to try the nearest light switch. 'What's this wi' the candles? Can we no' have a proper light on?' He sat down again, the candle flickers accentuating the lines of disgruntlement on his thrawn, skinny face.

Richard was now, even by topers' standards, fairly drunk — certainly by non-drinkers' norms. 'Fond memories this, Your Grace? MI5, eh? All this whispering, what? Bit rude, lads, in front of the ladies. Remember what Morag and Mhairi said, you informed me…?' Richard, with a smile, prompted his two chums.

'Youse are ignorant pigs, so youse ur!' The trio trilled, fluted and screeched, if not in harmony, at least in unison.

United again.

'No' bad, Richard, you're coming along,' a suddenly cheerier Jack conceded. 'Now mimic one o' the servants and get some sauce. Never mind, get it myself… if I have to scoff stone-cold suppers, I'll need brown sauce.' Jacky stood again and raked through various tall, imposing glass cabinets to no avail.

'Hey, Jacky!' Brian shouted loudly, as Jacky was by now some considerable distance away, rummaging at the far end of the long room. 'What's the party line on servants *vis-à-vis* their aristocratic employers?'

'It's quite simple: the aristocracy are a corrupt and thankfully decaying corpus of parasites that lives off the surplus of the productive classes. Objective truth. That's all. That's hit!'

Richard was not only drunk but a tad foolish and not a little brave as he shouted at a distant Jacky:

'From an unemployed economist!'

'To an overpaid accountant! And as for the servant class: they are every bit as parasitic. And as reactionary. Like you and Thatcher. You deserve each other. Like Alec and... Tony Blair... Like... no bloody brown sauce.' Jacky fell silent, but continued to rummage loudly.

'Plato argues — *The Dialogues*, I think it is...' Richard began, just loudly enough for Jacky to hear and kick-start the little man's long tirade.

'Stick Plato up your arse! Plato was only justifying a slave-owning class of parasites that included himself. His puny answer to the Heraclitean flux and Cratylus's Wagging Finger. You'll be telling me next that Beauty Art and Science can only come from a privileged leisure class!' Jacky screamed, then laughed scornfully as he pointed back at Neville's prostrate head that might have been sleeping or eating. Or both. 'Can you see Neville there, Duke of Etcetera, integrating Relativity with Magnetic Field Theory? My arse. Your buttox. He cannae even find the friggin' salt. And, what use is all this crystal without brown sauce?'

Brian grabbed the guitar and did a very competent burst of *The Crystal Chandeliers*.

'Oh, the crystal chandeliers
Light up the paintings on the wall,
The marble statuettes
Are standing stately in the hall...'

Jacky continued to shout over Brian's singing. 'Your trouble, Richard, is you and your type read all the same books, think all the same thoughts and say all the same

171

things. You define Knowledge and Reason as what you think you know and what you think reasonable.' He now had to bawl over the music: '*All right thinking men*, the cry o' the mediocre, every one of you to the last. English!'

Richard went to reply several times, but was forced to wait until both Brian's belting it out and Jacky's bellowing over stopped. With slow majestic dignity, Richard rose.

'I've taken quite enough, Jack, of your emotional diarrhoea. And your intellectual constipation. I am not by nature combative. On principle I eschew personal assault — but I make an exception this one time. You, Jack, are capable of making Thorstein Veblen proselytise the Khmer Rouge. You also make John Prescott appear quite sane. I know I shall regret this later, but right now it must be said...' Richard stood shakily, drew a deep breath. 'Jack, you are the arch-typical epitome of your homeland. A whining, whinging junky subsidy who wants its oil and drinks it. A paranoia that knows no bounds. Except that of the Barnett Formula, of course. The carping Anglophobia, the puerile insularity, the Kailyard mentality, the delusions of adequacy, all that I can overlook. Indeed, I have lived with. And under. But what I cannot tolerate, for one moment longer, Jack, is your *inconsistency*. There. I've said it.'

'Sounds a serious charge, Jacky.' The words echoed as Brian spoke into the sound box of the otherwise now silent guitar.

'Could be.' Jacky had returned to the table and sat, muttering, 'Nae friggin' sauce.'

Neville suddenly sat up, a small cold chip dangling from his chin.

'Gosh. Never realised how famished I was. Thank you, lads. No more haggises, are there?' He deftly grabbed and popped the errant chip into his mouth.

'Haggii. Ya dumplin',' Jacky snorted.

'Jack, the argument for *haggii* is contingent upon it being declined like a Latin noun such as... say, Onus: Onus, Ona, Onum. Plural, Masculine. Onii. However...'

'Jesus, Mary and Joseph! I've heard it all now.' Brian was not feigning incredulity. 'When oor brickies come moaning to me about their bonuses, it's really their *bonii* that's upsetting them? That's the problem with a Scotvec in Building Technology — it leaves one feeling so inadequate. What a load of shite!'

'Shit,' Jacky said quietly.

'Shite.' Brian was even quieter.

'Shit! It was Richard that said it.'

'Shite! It was me that said it.'

'Shit! The content was Richard's.'

'That's shite!'

'No. Shit! Richard, being English, talks shit. We, being Scottish, talk...'

'Shite!' Brian and Jacky concluded together.

'By George, they've got it!' Neville exclaimed in an inadvertent but plausible pastiche of a legless Rex Harrison.

'Shit, shite, shite, shit,' a euphoric Richard sang, '*let's call the whole thing off.*'

They all drank cheerily in the resurrected happy atmosphere.

'Well.' Neville pushed the newspaper wrappings aside. 'That was certainly a meal to... and this' — he held up his crystal goblet of *Irn Bru* – 'this amber liquid. Quite unique.'

'*Irn Bru*, Your Grace,' Brian stated. 'It's for your other national sport: Sobering Up.'

After a long silence, broken only by a desultory burp or delicate fart, mostly from Neville, Richard lit a small cigar.

'It all brings back to me a picnic by the River Ouse. A scorching August. The pater drove us down in the old Alvis. It was my sister Celia's fourteenth birthday. We were both allowed our first glass of wine. A rather fine claret, as I recall.' He paused to muse, 'Wonder what ever happened to her?'

'Ah know the feeling, Richard,' Brian began. 'Wan mornin' after dinnertime, ah woke in this bird's bath. She climbs oot an' says: *An' ah suppose yae'll be wantin' breakfast*. A few minutes later, her heid comes roon the lavvy door: *Yae cannae huv it: nae butter*.'

After a long pause, Richard observed, 'Ah. Life.'

'Ah. Butter,' Jacky said, then paused to cackle. 'My defining moment was a pie-supper out of Giovenetti's.' He snorted in anticipation. 'I was sharin' it wi' a lassie called... call her Mary Stewart. Looked like Tuesday Weld. All those present who remember Tuesday Weld, put your hand under the table. We were oan this park bench. The world drifted by in a timeless fashion: Old Sammy

Gardner rakin' the bins for Embassy coupons; Creepy McSween the parky tryin' to see in the lassies' bog wi' his shavin' mirror on a stick. Tuesday and me were'nae saying much — it being oor first time dining al fresco, oor first time dining actually, when this wee dug, a scabby wee poodle it was, runs up behind this huge Alsatian and has the temerity to jump on and try the business. And Tuesday says sweetly: *Haw, wid ye luk at that?* And she starts tae laugh. I turned to her and smiled. As our eyes met, laughter bubbled up inside me with joy, but my mouth was full of pie and chips. So, to be polite, to impress Mary, I laughed with my lips pressed tight together. And a great big green rubbery snotter landed right on top of our...' Jacky paused. 'Oh, did I ever tell you, as a boy I was plagued with catarrh? You'll no' be wantin' the rest o' these chips, then?'

'Maybe you could spare me some?' a disembodied male voice boomed.

A big, burly police sergeant, followed by a petite woman police constable, came in to the room, slowly surveying the scene before them; the woman apparently looking for something in particular as she bent to look under the table, before rising and nodding to her sergeant.

'Oh! No. So soon?' Neville seemed horrified, quickly saddened, then cowed. 'All right, I'll get my... my things. It's a fair cop. I'll come quietly. Bang to rights.'

'I'll handle this, don't say a word, Jack — only exacerbate things.' A very tipsy, angered Richard faced the police to speak over Neville's pathetic obsequiousness.

'What is this? Intrusion. You can't just... without invitation... altogether quite unacceptable...'

The sergeant in particular seemed amused, a tight smile flickering on his full bloated lips. 'An *Englishman's* castle is his home? Is that it? Well, this is Brodick and...'

'Precisely!' Richard spluttered, but grew increasingly flustered thereafter. 'No... look, there seems to be... some confusion, officer.' He made towards the sergeant, but the woman constable stopped him with a grasp on his arm with her tiny hand. Richard looked down on her. 'Unhand me, you lout. Loutess...'

'Pansy, take these two, an' be gentle on Tosh; remember his age... and condition,' the sergeant instructed.

'Aye, serge. Right, Tosh, you ken where the van is. Make yerself snug while I see to your toff companion.'

'Tosh?' Richard outraged. 'Yes, it is tosh. *Tosh* is what this is! Damned unadulterated impertinent tosh! Tosh? Are you blind, my man... girl...? That's Neville, the Duke of Arran. I don't think you quite understand with whom you are dealing... His Grace shall...'

'His Grace?' The sergeant did a wonderful impression of the archetypal laughing policeman. He recovered slowly. 'Tosh converted *and* promoted...? Huckle him, Pansy!'

Richard adopted what a Scottish martial artist manqué would term the *canny-catch-me* stance and ran round the table, followed by WPC Pansy. He suddenly tripped over the rucksack left by Morag and Mhairi. As Pansy collared Richard, the sergeant bent and started to inspect some of the spilled contents of the rucksack. He struggled to his formidable, fat, flat feet holding a small, exotic-looking fuchsia-type shrub. He handled it carefully and protectively as if it were a newborn, the polythene-wrapped root ball perhaps reminiscent to him of a filled nappy.

Pansy dragged Richard to his feet, despite Richard's struggle and nursing the ankle that had struck the solid rucksack.

'You're huckled!' Thus, Pansy read Richard his Scottish Rights. (Even if she had been christened 'Miranda', this is still all he would have got.)

'Huckled? Huckled?' Richard, even in personal crisis, was a stickler for full cognitive literary comprehension. 'Jack... eh, *huckled* is...? Unhand me or I'll... Jack, Jack, see that, this?... Police brutality. You're right... police state. Just wait until independence. *Huckled*?'

Richard was huckled over the room by WPC Pansy as Jacky adopted what Richard would later claim was a *nothing-to-do-with-me s*tance.

The sergeant carefully lifted the rucksack onto the table, depositing it safely on some of the more empty newspapers. He carefully extracted another half dozen small shrubs from the rucksack, each, as the first, exotic-looking and complete with protective polythene diaper. 'Hold him there, Pansy!' he barked. Pansy now had Richard at the door.

The sergeant returned to his discoveries. 'What have we here, then? One: one Fuchsia — *corymbiflora/procubens* hybrid. Very rare. Two: one pseudo but hardy orchid — *Terrestrial cypripedium*, complete with expensive osmunda fibre. Very sensible, very professional.' He looked apparently kindly at Jacky and Brian. 'I knew that Open University course would come in handy: *Shrubbing for Sergeants*. Three: one *stransvergia*. *Stransvergia Strathalbyn!* Scotland's one and only! Twenty years in the breeding. Bred and fed and reared in loving Brodick Castle's caring gardens and...' He suddenly looked very stern.

'Offences against the Trees, Woodlands and Shrubs Preservation (Scotland) Act, perchance? Not to be sniffed at, wi' global warming an' the plight o' the minky whale an' what have you...' He turned again and spoke directly to Jacky and Brian: 'Right, lads, keep your arses parked and see if we can come up wi' a reasonable story. An' remember Occam's Razor: nothing too elaborate, eh?'

Jacky and Brian sat examining the displayed contents of the rucksack, then looked at each other for inspiration. Then they looked over at Richard, who stood waiting for salvation and release from the secure up-the-back arm-hold of the tiny policewoman, who was stretching to her tip-toes to make it.

'I'm very disappointed in you, Richard,' Jacky said sadly, shaking his head slowly.

'An' you an English gentleman, too. Who would've believed it?' Brian also shook his head at Richard, then the sergeant, now seated alongside him.

Richard's spluttered protests reverberated in the hall as, after a nod from the sergeant, Pansy swiftly huckled him out and away.

The sergeant now appeared to be further examining the rescued plants on the table, but he suddenly exclaimed: 'Here! That widnae be the remnants of haggii suppers, wid it?'

Brian pushed a newspaper wrapping towards the sergeant.

'Oh, thanks; it's Brian, isn't it? You're the golfer. Big Alec said you were.' The sergeant took a bite of a greasy, battered, half-eaten haggis. 'Mmh,' he laughed in appreciation, 'just like the revenge — best served cold, eh, boys?' He lifted the nearest beer can and spurted it open. 'Had you down for that real ale pish, but ah'm warmin' to you. Okay?'

'Ola kala, sergeant, ola kala,' Brian added, as the sergeant supped greedily, contentedly.

Chapter 31

They're no' awa... just tae leave ye

The two women were on a bench on the lower deck of the late Sunday afternoon ferry back from Brodick to Ardrossan.

'Oh well, Rag, I suppose it did have its compensations. Though not exactly what we had in mind. Still, lucky I spotted the police torches in the castle gardens while I was waiting for Non-Action Man in our boudoir.'

'You know, Vas, in an ideal world we would have had a good time, having found all the plants and shrubs on our hit list, returned to our sweet little dealer and been mightily paid. Well, at least paid enough for two weeks on a real holiday island. The yob-free side of Mustique, mayhaps.'

'In an ideal world you would have re-discovered the romance of youth. You know the sort of thing: where that Brian fellow has been transformed from a callow and crude youth into an educated, polished and sophisticated, strikingly handsome and virile hunk of a man. You would have both danced off into the sunset.'

'Virile, polished, handsome and *rich*. But it was not to be. Still, as you say, it had its moments. You know, Vas, I think it does one good to meet people like Brian and that little whatever his name was. It makes you appreciate what you have in life. Stops you hankering after what is all a chimera; destroys the romantic delusions one might ever have harboured for the lower classes. God, I can hardly wait to get back: Buchanan Galleries and Princes Square look out, I feel a serious bout of Glasgow retail therapy coming on.

'May even pay for some of it, too.'

'*Moi aussi.*'

They looked at each other and, with a smile, together said:

'That's French!'

They were still laughing as they wandered arm-in-arm to the rail on the bay side of the ship.

Richard and Jacky appeared on the upper deck.

Richard had his right arm in a sling and the beginnings of a black and yellow left eye. His right eye had a plaster above the eyebrow.

They walked to the dockside rail and looked down for some time in silence. Richard was vaguely aware that his peculiar fear of water was absent, but somehow, right at this moment, the discovery was inconsequential, and being cured was strangely unimportant.

Some time later, four legs belonging to two people with their heads and shoulders shrouded by a blanket came into view and with great difficulty staggered their way through the late-morning stragglers towards the ferry, a few ground-feeding gulls squawking in protest at the interruption to their late morning snacks. Elevenses for gulls.

Through the descending darkness and slight haar, Richard could see that there appeared to be some considerable activity made by the two heads under the coarse, grey blanket. At the foot of the gangplank, the four legs stopped. The blanket slipped away to reveal Brian and Pansy, the WPC, in plain yet attractive clothes, in full kiss. They separated swiftly, but Pansy reached up on tip-toes to grab Brian's ears, to give him one, final, strong hug and long kiss.

The ship's tannoy announced its imminent departure. Pansy, with a sad, last, long look at Brian, turned on her heel, leaving Brian to mount the gangplank. In his left hand he held his battered holdall. From his right dangled a pair of police handcuffs.

The three men were now looking over the upper deck rail as the ferry made many more imminent and urgent departure noises, the car deck now closing with a few creaks and a final clang.

Brian honked discreetly over the rail and turned to the other two, breathing deeply with satisfaction:

'Ah, that's better. Whit about Pansy? What a cracker.' He rubbed his ribs, then his lower back. 'She took the best o' three falls. She's quite romantic with it.' He removed the handcuffs on his right wrist. 'Gave me a wee keepsake. And did you see the way she held the blanket over my head to the gangway. That's a woman who understands male pride. Compare and contrast wi' Morag and Mhairi. Jacky, you were right about them, by the way: nae class. I mean, who in their right minds would want to nick plants and shrubs? I had the impression that they were trying too hard to be better than they really were. You know, as if they were from Airdrie or Coatbridge pretending to be Lower Dennistoun. And what about that sergeant? Man's a beast, drinkin' like that. Should be locked up.'

'Well, he was eventually. Shared Richard's cell. Didnae appear too happy about it, either.' Jacky looked pointedly at Richard's injuries.

A long silence was broken as ever by Jacky.

'Would you look at it?' Jacky laughed scornfully as he viewed the dock and shore. '*Scotland in Miniature.* More like: *Arran — The Arsehole o' the World.* They'll never get me back in a million years.'

'It'll be somewhat later than that for me, Jack.' Richard winced, gently touching his plastered eyebrow.

'Well, you're barred anyway now, Richard. But for me there was a time when Arran stood for the best that was Scotland; quintessentially Scottish.' Jacky paused, looking out at the starting drizzle that attempted to dissipate the haar. 'Golf? And I never got to swing a club in anger. What a dump.' He turned away from the obscuring view, his bile on the boil now. 'But I don't suppose that'll bother you, Brian. 'S good that one of us got a game in. Even if it might just be his last in his homeland. Germany! Golf in Germany. You a club pro? An' I like the way you broke it to me last night. *Oh, by the way, ah'm off tae Germany tae be a club pro.* Just like that. No thought to our series. Anyway, it was shite. No thought to my handicap. Scotland on the verge of momentous decisions and you jump ship. Just as selfish as that shite-bag Alec. Didn't even put in an appearance. New Labour: auld tricks. Golf mates? Huh!'

'Don't go on about that game, eh? The boys at the Loundesdale were a man short: what could I say? Big Alec had put it about that I could play a bit... anyway, it was a really weird experience, you know, playing sober. Really strange, having tae concentrate: never realised golf was such a tricky game. Mair fun, actually. The German thing's been on the cards for some time: nothin' here to keep me. You've got Kathy an' the weans an' the people at the broo every week. Richard's got his... What have you got, Richard?'

'At the risk of sounding maudlin, I thought that I had friends, boon companions united and divided in the theatre of war that is, that was, our fourball series. Jack, Alex and yourself: that's all, Brian.' Richard looked to be on the point of real tears, then shuddered at the relief he had experienced with Jacky having to perform the driving on to the ferry. He would need to drive all three home from Ardrossan now, given Richard's suspected broken arm.

'You're right, Richard. That is maudlin,' Jacky agreed.

'Richard, we should charge for you this weekend,' Brian suggested. 'Nearly learning the language, and definitely getting some street and party-cred. You'll have them spellbound and open-legged at your soirees now. Banged-up straight from the felon's mooth... A *swally* to expire for.'

Jacky had returned to the rail and now looked down to roar, 'What's keepin' this boat? Come on, get the gangplank up or whatever you do, will you? Ah want out of here, pronto!'

As if in response, some children's chanting started up. At first it was indecipherable, but those cognate with the Scottish vernacular singing of underage children would have instantly identified the unpleasant and aggressive tone.

Richard, however, went over to look down for the source.

'Ah, look, Jack, a visiting school party. How charming to see that the youth of today retain such innocent pleasures.' He began to sing to the tune of Marie's Wedding: '*Step we gaily off we go, hum, hum, hum, hum, toe on toe*', only to be stopped by the wind-borne snatches from the children on the dock:

'*Oh, Flower of Scotland, When will we hear that shite again?... Hey! Macleod! Get affa ma ewe!*'

'That's not... no... What are they singing?... Doesn't sound like any walking song that I...'

'Walking song? *Happy Wanderer*? Falder feckin' ee? Naw, it's the Ardrossan equivalent of the Hakka. 'S called the Fucku. It's traditional. Here, ah'll show you the traditional reply. Right, Jacky?'

Jacky and Brian leaned over the rail to make the traditional hand and arm gestures signifying *Get it right up ye!* accompanied by curses and imprecations that were apposite. Richard was discomfited and embarrassed, but Brian and even Jacky were now a bit happier. The singing died off abruptly.

'They'll need a fair dose o' counsellin' after that. Excuse me, chaps.' Brian moved to the bay-side rail and honked copiously.

'His manners have improved a lot,' Jacky drily commented to Richard.

'Good Christ in a leotard!' Morag screamed, before almost instantly regressing to 'Ya dirty bastard, ye!' A dripping Morag and a previously grinning but now scowling Mhairi looked up, seeking the source of the vomit. They saw three faces looking down.

'Not so clean yerself! You've got vomit in yer hair!' Jacky shouted, before joining Brian in a hasty retreat.

This left Richard leaning over the rail. He should have been expert in the art of placation in the many proximate aftermaths of Jacky, sometimes Brian, but perhaps forty-eight hours on Arran, five Richard years-worth of alcohol, six hours in the over-physical company of a drunken, decidedly Anglophobic policeman in a locked prison cell would account for his pathetic rationalised attempt at appeasement:

'Seagulls.'

'Seagulls!' Mhairi upped her dander in support of her victimised soul sister. 'I'll tell you whit tae dae wi' yer seagulls: ye can…'

Her pointed suggestion was drowned out by the ferry's hooter and the tannoy inviting non-passengers to get off or else.

Richard joined Brian and Jacky at the dockside rail as they both stared wearily into the far distance. Richard, still worrying about his pusillanimous avian-centred explanation to the ladies, nevertheless spotted something among the frantic movements on the quayside.

'I say, Jack, Brian... that's not...? Look, over there by the Tourist Office... No...?'

'In the Pringle sweater and the hello-sailor bunnet... reading the paper, with the…' Brian observed.

'The blonde on his arm? Naw,' Jacky concluded.

'It's not really like him, is it? Say it isn't,' Richard demanded.

'No' really. Just the gear he's wearing. And the mobile phone. And the white *Alpha Romeo*. What d'you think, Jacky?'

'The sleekit big... an' wi' a bird. On Paradise Island, tae? Christ, he looks really happy as well.' Jacky paused but briefly. 'Know what? He'll kick himself if he thinks he's missed us.'

'Would never forgive himself. Never. Would he, Jacky?' Brian rhetoricalised.

'Hold that thing; hey you! Aye, you! Get that gangplank back. Hold that gangplank!' Jacky commanded downwards to the uber-busy deckhands. 'Hey, Alec! Wait for us! It's us! It's your pals!'

'Ola kola! Ola kola, Alec!' Brian shouted out, as they hit the top deck stairs and just avoided the two angry women struggling their way up.

The ferry just started to move as Richard, still at the rail, saw his erstwhile friends leap onto the quay.

'Alex! Jack! Brian!' He leaned out on to the rail and put his serviceable hand to his ear. 'What's that, Jack?

Can't hear you. My back? Just a mild twinge. What? Behind me? What about it?' He turned.

Morag clumped and Mhairi trotted at him from his rear.

His lack of life, then thoughts of his car, his golf equipment and his luggage deep in the bows flashed before him just as his leap hit the water.

The two ladies stared down over the rail, apparently indifferent to the cries from the sea.

'Help, help. I can't swim. Mayday! Mayday!'

'*M'aidez, m'aidez*?' Mhairi mused to Morag.

'That's French!' Morag shouted down.

'Nae class. Nae class at aw,' they agreed in unison.

END.